"Does the ring fit?"

Rad slid it over her finger and the feel of his hand holding hers, the way he bent his head to watch what he was doing, all seemed like images from a real engagement, from a man presenting the woman he loved with a token of his intentions to spend the rest of his life with her.

Serena swallowed the sudden lump in her throat.

The ring fit.

Perfectly.

Her eyes met his. The intensity she saw there caught her by surprise.

Then he smiled and said, "Mission accomplished."

If his mission had been to invade her heart, it looked like he was succeeding.

Dear Reader,

From a Texas sweetheart to a Chicago advice columnist, our heroines will sweep you along on their journeys to happily ever after. Don't miss the tender excitement of Silhouette Romance's modern-day fairy tales!

In *Carolina's Gone A' Courting* (SR #1734), Carolina Brubaker is on a crash course with destiny—and the man of her dreams—*if* she can survive their summer of forced togetherness! Will she lasso the heart of her ambitious rancher? Find out in the next story in Carolyn Zane's THE BRUBAKER BRIDES miniseries.

To this once-burned plain Jane a worldly, sophisticated, handsome lawyer is *not* the kind of man she wants...but her heart has other plans. Be there for the transformation of this no-nonsense woman into the beauty she was meant to be, in *My Fair Maggy* (SR #1735) by Sharon De Vita.

Catch the next installment of Cathie Linz's miniseries MEN OF HONOR, *The Marine Meets His Match* (SR #1736). His favorite independent lady has agreed to play fiancée for this military man who can't resist telling her what to do. If only he could order her to *really* fall in love....

Karen Rose Smith brings us another emotional tale of love and family with *Once Upon a Baby...* (SR #1737). This love-leery sheriff knows he should stay far away from his pretty and pregnant neighbor—he's not the husband and father type. But delivering her baby changes everything....

I hope you enjoy every page of this month's heartwarming lineup!

Mavis C. Allen
Associate Senior Editor

Please address questions and book requests to:
Silhouette Reader Service
U.S.: 3010 Walden Ave., P.O. Box 1325, Buffalo, NY 14269
Canadian: P.O. Box 609, Fort Erie, Ont. L2A 5X3

The Marine Meets His Match

CATHIE LINZ

MEN
OF
HONOR

SILHOUETTE *Romance* ®

Published by Silhouette Books

America's Publisher of Contemporary Romance

For all the booksellers who have supported me over the years, including Judi Brownfield and Ellen Fryer from Books at Sunset (whose bookstore inspired my heroine's store), Maureen Greene from Borders Books, Kathy Baker from Waldenbooks, Cindi Streicher from Waldenbooks, Betty Schulte and the gang from Paperback Outlet, and Sharon Murphy from everywhere <grin>—to name just a few. Your enthusiastic handselling has made all the difference in the world, and I appreciate your hard work more than I can say!

Acknowledgment:
Special thanks to United States Marine Corps family Susan and Harry Frank for answering my many dumb questions. Any artistic license that I may have used is my idea and my fault, not theirs. *Semper Fi!*

 SILHOUETTE BOOKS

ISBN 0-373-19736-5

THE MARINE MEETS HIS MATCH

Visit Silhouette Books at www.eHarlequin.com

Printed in U.S.A.

Books by Cathie Linz

Silhouette Romance

One of a Kind Marriage #1032
*Daddy in Dress Blues #1470
*Stranded with the Sergeant #1534
*The Marine & the Princess #1561
A Prince at Last! #1594
*Married to a Marine #1616
**Sleeping Beauty & the
    Marine* #1637
*Her Millionaire Marine #1720
**Cinderella's Sweet-Talking
    Marine* #1727
**The Marine Meets His
    Match* #1736

Silhouette Books

Montana Mavericks
"Baby Wanted"

*Men of Honor
†Three Weddings and a Gift

Silhouette Desire

Change of Heart #408
A Friend in Need #443
As Good as Gold #484
Adam's Way #519
Smiles #575
Handyman #616
Smooth Sailing #665
Flirting with Trouble #722
Male Ordered Bride #761
Escapades #804
Midnight Ice #846
Bridal Blues #894
A Wife in Time #958
†Michael's Baby #1023
†Seducing Hunter #1029
†Abbie and the Cowboy #1036
Husband Needed #1098

CATHIE LINZ

left her career in a university law library to become a *USA TODAY* bestselling author of contemporary romances. She is the recipient of the highly coveted Storyteller of the Year Award given by *Romantic Times* and was nominated for a Love and Laughter Career Achievement Award for the delightful humor in her books.

Although Cathie loves to travel, she is always glad to get back home to her family, her various cats, her trusty computer and her hidden cache of Oreo cookies!

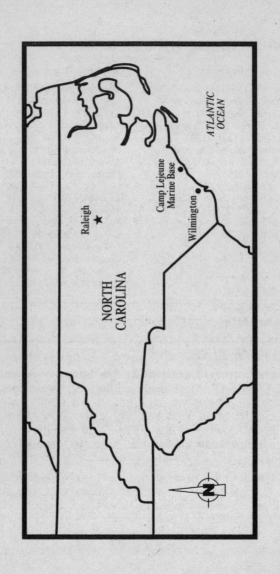

ATLANTIC OCEAN

Camp Lejeune Marine Base

Wilmington

Raleigh

NORTH CAROLINA

Chapter One

"Discipline is a critical part of being a Marine and of succeeding in life. Without discipline there's chaos. Marines do *not* like chaos." U.S. Marine Captain Rad Kozlowski narrowed his eyes, his stare drilling into those few who dared look him in the face. "Chaos indicates a lack of discipline. A lack of willpower. These are not things that will be tolerated in the United States Marine Corps. I want to make that perfectly clear."

Rad paused for emphasis. "But for those few who can make the grade, the reward is great. Not the financial reward. I'm not talking about money here." He had an expressive voice and he made good use of it. His inflection was powerful, his delivery one step below barking orders. "I'm talking about being part of a brotherhood with values like honor, courage, commitment. The United States Marine Corps is not for every-one. Because only a few have what it takes to be part of this elite fighting force. Understood?"

The fifth-grade class at Kennedy Middle School nod-ded solemnly.

"Uh, thank you, Captain Kozlowski." Mrs. Simp-son, the teacher who'd organized the event, sounded a tad nervous. "We appreciate you coming in today for our Career Day and speaking to the class."

"No problem, ma'am. I was glad to do it."

Not true. Rad hadn't joined the Marine Corps to speak to a bunch of rug rats. But when duty called, he always answered. Even when he thought it was dumb and a waste of his time.

"Does anyone have any questions for Captain Koz-lowksi? No? Well, then, Captain, thanks again."

Rad recognized his cue to leave and headed for the nearest exit. He left the gymnasium by a side door. Once out in the Carolina sunshine of a late September day, he paused a moment to take a deep breath.

He smelled her perfume a second before he saw her. The long-legged blonde wearing a red dress. She'd stood at the back during his presentation.

"Congratulations, Captain." Her mocking comment was not intended to be a compliment. "You managed to scare a bunch of ten-year-olds. Does that make you happy?"

"Deep-dish pizza and cold beer make me happy, ma'am." Sexy blondes like her also made him happy. Rad completed a quick visual check of her assets— long golden hair gathered up into a ponytail, lush lips, high cheekbones that gave her a ritzy look, big green eyes.

She was tall, just a few inches shorter than his six foot one height, and the dress she wore displayed an incredible pair of legs. A breeze lifted the hemline, granting him a tempting glimpse of her tanned thighs.

Oh, yeah, blondes like her *definitely* topped his list of things that made him happy. Maybe this day wasn't a total waste after all.

Rad flashed her a smile.

She tossed him a dismissive look laced with disapproval. "Don't you think you were a little intense in there?"

"Marines are intense."

"And competitive."

"Affirmative, ma'am. And your interest in all this would be?"

"I'm a bookseller."

"A bookseller named…?"

"Serena. Serena Anderson. I spoke earlier this afternoon for the Career Day event."

"I'm sorry I missed it."

"So am I. Maybe then you would have done your speech differently."

"I doubt that, ma'am."

"You could have been a little more approachable."

His smile widened. "I can be very approachable when the situation warrants it. Like now. How would you like to discuss this further over a cold drink?"

"I wouldn't like that at all."

"Why not?"

The sexy Marine clearly wasn't accustomed to having his invitations turned down, Serena noted. He might have intimidated the entire fifth-grade class, but there was no way he was going to steamroller over her.

True, he'd made Serena's heart beat faster without even trying and now that he was trying, well... He was good, she'd give him that. The gleam in his brown eyes let her know this was a man used to having his way with women.

She could understand why. He was the kind of man who got noticed. And not just because of the impressive Marine dress blue uniform he was wearing, or the confident way he carried himself. Living as she did so close to Camp Lejeune in North Carolina, she'd seen plenty of Marines.

But this one was different.

He'd gotten under her skin.

At first she'd told herself it was because of the way he'd talked to the kids as if they were recruits in his command. He was definitely a man accustomed to giving orders and having them instantly obeyed.

Serena was definitely a woman who didn't respond well to being bossed around. She'd experienced enough of that to last her a lifetime.

Maybe she wouldn't have reacted so strongly were it not for the fact that her goddaughter Becky was in that group he'd just spoken to. And his forceful voice had made the shy Becky almost dive under her chair in the back row. Serena had been standing directly behind her at the time. Only Serena's soothing hands on the little girl's trembling shoulders had kept her in her seat.

So Serena had waited out here to confront him, to tell him that kids needed special care.

Instead of agreeing, he'd stuck to his guns.

That figured. How like a man, especially a bossy man.

"You're not married are you?" he suddenly asked, his gaze sliding to her left hand.

"Absolutely not!"

So the blonde had a thing against marriage. Rad could relate. He was no big fan himself. Despite the fact that his two older brothers had gotten tied down with wives, Rad was in no hurry to surrender his freedom. He was in a hurry to get to know her better, however. "What's the problem then?"

"There are too many for me possibly to go into them all." Her voice was tart.

"Pick just a few then."

"You know the things that work for you as a Marine? Traits like being arrogant and bossy?"

The seductive bookseller was trying to push his buttons. He wondered why. "We prefer to think of those traits as confidence and leadership."

"These are not traits I respond well to."

"And why is that?"

His direct gaze and calm question flustered her. "I've got my reasons, okay?"

"Okay. When you know me better, you can tell me what they are."

She blinked at him, her dark eyelashes fluttering against her creamy skin. Not that he was a guy who normally noticed a female's eyelashes, but she had such great eyes. And legs. And breasts.

The sizzle of attraction was strong. Stronger than he'd felt in a very long time. And it wasn't one-sided. Despite her words, the lightning flashes of chemistry were definitely reciprocated.

Like now, when her gaze got all tangled-up with his. The male-female message was there. The awareness, the temptation. The sparks, the struggle. She licked her lush lips before finally looking away.

"I'm not going to get to know you better, Captain." Her voice was breathless and abrupt but emphatic. "Goodbye."

He watched her hurry away, appreciating the sway of her hips. He remembered a song that had been big a while back, something about a *Lady in Red*. She was like poetry in motion, the way she moved. Southern women had a natural way of doing that, making a man take notice. But he hadn't detected a local accent when she'd spoken.

Still, if she'd spoken at this school today, she had to live nearby. The tote bag she carried had an open-book design and a bookstore name on it: The Reader's Place—Home Of Novel Ideas.

He had plenty of novel ideas about her. All of them steamy. He had to get back to the base now, but tomorrow, he'd make a stop at her bookstore. Because Rad was not a man who gave up easily. He wasn't a man who gave up at all.

He was still thinking about Serena when he returned to Camp Lejeune. Which was why he didn't see Heidi Burns until it was too late.

The general's eighteen-year-old daughter was a beauty with her dark hair and big blue eyes. She was also a pain in the keister.

The general's daughter had been making Rad's life difficult for several weeks now. Which was how he'd ended up with that school assignment. Not his usual type of mission.

When Rad hadn't accepted Heidi's invitation to go out with her, she'd warned him that she'd go to her daddy to get what she wanted if necessary. He hadn't believed her. Then his CO had given him the school assignment, saying the "request" had come from the general himself.

Rad knew he had to do something about this situation. Heidi had decided she wanted him. Not that he'd ever given her one iota of attention. Well, okay, so he'd smiled at her when he'd first met her. But that was it. She claimed to have fallen in love with him on sight.

Staying out of her way was difficult, because she followed him like a lost puppy. She was daddy's princess who could do no wrong. Spoiled all her life, she'd always gotten what she wanted.

Now she wanted Rad.

"There you are." She grasped his arm. "You, like, have to join Daddy and me for dinner tonight."

"I'm sorry. I can't do that."

"Why not?" Her expression warned him that he'd better have a good reason and that no reason would be good enough.

There was only one thing he could think of saying. "My fiancée wouldn't approve."

That stopped Heidi in her tracks. For barely a second. Then she laughed. "You don't have a fiancée."

"Yes, I do."

Heidi was no fool. She clearly suspected something was up. "Then why haven't you mentioned her before?"

"We just recently got engaged."

"What's her name?" She shot the question at him

with machine-gun speed, rattling him with her dogged persistence.

"Serena. Serena Anderson." The words were out of his mouth before he could stop them. "She's a bookseller."

"The building sold?" Serena looked at the Realtor removing the For Sale sign from the front.

"That's right. The new owner wants to meet with you later today, between five and six."

"About renewing my lease?"

"I'm assuming so, yes."

Serena felt as if she'd swallowed a swarm of bees. Nerves jangled in her stomach.

A yellow butterfly fluttered over the red petunias in the store's window boxes before floating away without a care in the world. What a life. She wondered what it would be like to be so free of worries, free of debt, free period.

Yes, but butterflies had problems too. They had to be careful or they'd end up splat on some car's windshield.

First bees, now butterflies. She was clearly on some kind of insect train of thought here. And such cheerful thoughts they were, too. She grimaced.

She didn't consider herself to be the over-anxious type. If asked to describe herself, she'd say she was good with people, that she'd worked hard over the years to try to find the good in the bad, and that she could be bribed with Belgian chocolate. Dark chocolate.

The distant rumble of thunder meant that Serena could cross watering the flowers off her list of things to do today.

Before entering her store, she paused a moment for her daily ritual—brushing her fingers against the lettering on the glass door. This was her dream come true.

Her bookstore, The Reader's Place, was located on the main floor of the three-story brick building. The second floor had a one-bedroom apartment, which she also rented. Another apartment, exactly like hers, was on the top floor.

When she'd found the location she'd known it was the perfect place, and had signed the one-year leases the same day for both the retail space and for the apartment.

A new owner most likely meant an increase in her rent. The question was, by how much? She was barely squeaking by as it was.

Her stomach shifted and did that buzzing-bee dance thing she hated. Thunder rumbled again just as a streak of sunlight beamed down on her. Find the silver lining. Maybe the new owner would be great. Maybe he'd leave the rents exactly as they were. Maybe he'd buy some books while he was there. It could happen.

"Did you forget your keys?" The question came from Jane Washington. She and her husband, Hosea, owned the florist shop in the building next door. In her early fifties, Jane's mocha skin had the youthful glow of a much younger woman.

"No, I was just thinking."

"Better do that inside," Jane advised. "There's a storm coming. I'll let you know if there are any weather advisories." Jane kept a radio on at all times. "There's a funny feeling in the air, like something big might happen."

"Something big did happen. Someone bought my building."

"Is that good news or bad?"

"I don't know yet. I'll find out later today when the new owner stops by."

"What are you doing standing out here?" This time the question came from Serena's assistant, Kalinda Patel. The nineteen-year-old college student had long black hair and beautiful dark brown eyes. She also had the look of someone who needed coffee…badly. "The cappuccino machine is inside and I need my caffeine."

Lightning flashed as if emphasizing Kalinda's statement. "Okay, okay, I'm going inside." Quickly unlocking the door, Serena walked into her pride and joy—her bookstore.

While Kalinda hurried to set up the cappuccino machine behind the counter for her morning drink, Serena flipped on the lights and looked around. Serena's imprint was everywhere. She'd helped build the bookcases alongside the handyman she'd hired. She'd found the pair of comfy reading chairs at a local Goodwill store and had sewn the chintz slipcovers herself. They framed the entrance to the romance section, one of her bestselling areas.

Beyond that was the alcove housing the mystery section. Mock yellow-and-black plastic crime scene ribbons lined the shelves. A vintage movie poster of Basil Rathbone as Sherlock Holmes in *The Hound of the Baskervilles* hung on the wall.

The science fiction section was next, with *Star Wars* posters and signed covers from authors who had visited her store. Nearby she'd just recently started a young adult section with a variety of selections for adolescents. The area where westerns were shelved was relatively small, but very homey with a twig chair covered with a Native American woven blanket.

The children's section was tucked into an alcove and featured inviting beanbag chairs and a colorful alphabet area rug. Some of the shelves were lower and many of the books were positioned face out. She changed the posters every month—Dr. Seuss's *Cat in the Hat* had the central place of honor at the moment. That still left room for *Olivia the Pig* to one side and Sandra Boynton's latest to the other side.

In the far corner at the front of the store was the reading nook where Serena set her author appearances. A right-angled corner pine bench with vintage needlepoint pillows appeared to be built into the shelves all around it. She'd deliberately made this area look like a home library, placing classic books like *Pride and Prejudice* along with framed photos on the shelves.

A selection of handmade gift items, including scented candles and potpourri, were tucked in various nooks and crannies around the store.

The Reader's Place focused primarily on fiction, although she did carry some of the bestselling nonfiction titles, especially self-help books which were very popular with her customers.

Serena made a mental note that she needed to update the display of mass market paperback bestsellers, and do something with an autumnal theme for the Weekly Spotlight otherwise known as a metal baker's rack in its previous lifetime. It was also time to place her weekly book order with Ingram's and to pull returns to make room before the rush of new holiday titles arrived.

"Ah." The moan of delight came from Kalinda as she

sipped her drink. "Now I can face another day. Speaking of days, how did that Career Day thing go at the school?"

"There was a Marine there."

"I thought you were speaking to fifth-graders."

"I was."

Kalinda frowned. "Aren't they a little young to be recruited in the Marines?"

"He wasn't there to recruit them, he was there to talk about the Marine Corps."

"And judging from the expression on your face, you didn't approve of the way he did that."

"He was incredibly arrogant and bossy. When I told him that, he claimed to be displaying confidence and leadership skills."

"Hang on a second." Kalinda's dark eyes widened. "Did you say you told him he was arrogant and bossy?"

"Yes."

"And you lived to tell the tale?"

"He knew better than to mess with me."

Kalinda grinned. "Oh, yeah, I can see how a lean mean Marine would be scared spitless by a bodacious bookseller like you."

"I was wearing my red dress."

"Oh, well, that's different. You used your stealth weapon. Your sex appeal. You go, girl!" She gave Serena a high five.

"I did not use my sex appeal."

"Why not? Was he a dog?"

"No, he was extremely good-looking in a dark, brooding, sexy, gleam-of-wicked-humor, Adrian Paul kind of way."

"Adrian Paul!" Kalinda shrieked. "You found a guy who looks like Adrian Paul and you let him get away?"

"He was bossy and arrogant."

"So? Those are fixable things."

"Not always."

"You're thinking about your father, aren't you?"

Serena nodded. She hadn't told her assistant much about her past, just that her father was ex-military and extremely controlling. Her parents now lived in Las Vegas and Serena didn't see them very often.

"I can understand about impossible fathers. Mine is still demanding that I only date Indian men." Kalinda took another sip of her cappuccino. "Major bummer. Let's change the subject. Did the new order of category romances come in yet?"

"They arrived late yesterday afternoon after you left."

The rest of the day passed by quickly as it always did for Serena. A lot of her customers came in two or three times a week, allowing her to get to know them. She heard about their husband's jobs, their kids schooling, their problems and their triumphs. She also heard which books they loved.

Whenever a new customer arrived, Serena went out of her way to make them feel comfortable, in the hopes that they too would turn into a regular. Handselling was an important part of her job as she worked hard to unite readers with the books they were looking for, even if all she had to go on was, "It's a mystery with a red cover."

She deliberately tried to keep the thought of her impending meeting with the new building owner out of her thoughts. But once five o'clock rolled around, she couldn't help taking note of the time every few minutes.

The storm promised by the threatening thunder earlier in the day had skirted them without raining. Which meant Serena would have to water the store's window boxes today after all. She grabbed the plastic watering can and filled it with water from the washroom in the back. On Thursdays like today, she closed early, at five-thirty.

The bell on the door signaled her departure into the steamy heat outside. The petunias looked as wilted as she felt. *Think positive. Find the silver lining. Get chocolate...* Hmm, she did have a secret stash in the storeroom....

Turning, she bumped into a broad chest. "Sorry..." Her voice trailed off as she saw who was steadying her. Rad. Her pulse surged into overdrive, proving the point that her intense reaction to him the other day had not been a fluke. He wasn't even wearing his impressive dress blues uniform today. His blue jeans fit him to perfection as did the dark blue polo shirt he wore. "What are you doing here?"

"I came to talk to you."

"This isn't the time." She stepped away from him and held the watering can in front of her, as if it could protect her from the sex appeal he radiated. "I'm expecting someone any moment regarding an important business matter."

"I know. You're expecting me."

Jeez, the man was arrogant. "No, I'm not."

"Yes, you are." He followed her inside.

"I'm expecting the new owner of this building."

"That's right. That's me."

"But you're a Marine."

"Affirmative. A Marine with money. Not usual, I know. But I inherited a great deal of the green stuff from a Texas oil baron grandfather I barely knew."

She tried to make sense of what he was saying. "Why did you buy this building?"

"Because it's a good investment. And because I need your help."

"You bought the building because you need my help?"

"Affirmative. But then I always have been the radical one in my family."

Okay, clearly she needed to close early today. She flipped the sign from Open to Closed even though it was only five twenty-five and the store normally stayed open that night until five-thirty. This wasn't a conversation she could have in front of any customers. Luckily the store was empty and her assistant had already left for the day.

Serena got right to the point. "What about my lease?"

"I'll be glad to renew it at the present terms...if you help me out."

"If I do what you want, you mean?"

He nodded. "You help me and I'll help you."

Serena could see where this was going. "Well, you can forget it. I will not have sex with you!"

"Sex? Who said anything about sex? I don't want a lover, I want a fiancée. Or more accurately, someone who'll *pretend* to be my fiancée."

The mental light bulb finally went on. Serena had heard about the military's position about sexual orientation—don't ask, don't tell. She nodded understandingly. "I get it. You're gay."

"Gay?" Rad repeated incredulously. "I am not gay!" he growled before tugging her into his arms. The heat of his body permeated through the Indian cotton dress Serena wore. She was so close to him she could see the sherry-colored flecks in his brown eyes. Lowering his lips to just above hers, he whispered, "Want me to prove it to you?"

Chapter Two

Somehow Serena found the willpower to resist the temptation Rad presented. Hastily stepping away from him, she tried to keep her expression calm. "No, I don't want you to prove you're not gay. I'll take your word for it."

"What made you think I was?"

"You said you didn't want a lover, you wanted a fiancée."

"And that made you think I was gay?"

"It was a logical assumption."

"No, it wasn't."

She was about to argue with him over that fact when she realized that that's probably what he wanted. "Why don't you tell me *exactly* what it is you're proposing? Then I won't have to jump to conclusions."

"I'm *not* proposing."

"That was a figure of speech."

"Just so we're clear. What I need is a make-believe fiancée. Not the real thing."

"Why do you want someone to pose as your fiancée?"

"Because I'm having some trouble with the general's daughter Heidi."

"What did you do to her?"

"I didn't do anything. I smiled at her when I met her. That's about it."

"What's she done to you?"

"Made my life miserable. She's convinced she's fallen in love with me at first sight, which is ridiculous."

"It certainly is!"

Her instant and emphatic agreement shouldn't have irritated him, but it did. "You don't think a woman could fall for me?"

"I didn't say that. I said that falling in love with someone you don't know is ridiculous. She must not realize how arrogant and bossy you can be."

"She's a general's daughter. Her father is ten times bossier than I am. Clearly that's not a problem for her."

"It would be for me."

"Your father's not a general or something is he?" Rad demanded, his expression suddenly suspicious.

"No, my father has been out of the military for some time. He's in construction now."

"Is he the reason you have this thing against what you mistakenly perceive to be bossiness?"

There was no way she was confessing anything about her past to Rad. The less he knew about that part of her life the better. "Why don't we get back to your reasons for needing a fictional fiancée?"

"Fine. As I was saying, Heidi has been chasing me for several weeks now. When I didn't ask her out, she asked me. When I refused, politely of course, she warned me she was going to make my life difficult."

"What did she do?"

"For one thing, she got her father to give me that stupid assignment speaking at the middle school's Career Day."

His dismissal of the event irritated her greatly. "There was nothing stupid about the event. The only indication of a lack of judgment came when you spoke to the kids as if they were a bunch of recruits instead of children."

"At least they paid attention to me."

"And you're a man accustomed to being paid attention to."

"What's that supposed to mean?"

"Nothing. Go ahead. The general's daughter is making your life difficult."

"You don't understand. I can't afford to risk my military career by upsetting the spoiled daughter of a powerful general. So I came up with the idea of a fiancée. I figured that if I said I was engaged, then Heidi would back off."

"Why me?"

"Because Heidi caught me by surprise and your name slipped out."

"Slipped out?"

Rad nodded. "When she asked me for my fiancée's name. She cornered me as soon as I returned to the base after meeting you the other day. What are you smiling at?"

"The idea of a female cornering a big Marine like you. How old is this Heidi?"

"Eighteen. Why does that matter?"

"I was just curious, that's all."

"You'll probably get to meet her yourself pretty soon. It's only a matter of time before she comes here to check you out."

"So let me get this straight. You want me to pretend to be your fiancée to discourage Heidi from chasing you? For how long?"

"A few weeks. Until she loses interest."

"What if she doesn't?"

"She will."

"I don't know…. She sounds the determined type."

"Okay, then a few months. In return I'll cut your rent in half for the next year."

"Say that again?"

"You heard me."

"I'd need that to be in writing."

"I figured you would. So I had my attorney draw up a contract." He pulled it out of his back pocket.

The folded paper was still warm from his body heat. She tried to ignore that fact and focused on the legal terminology. While the length of the mock engagement had been left vague, the drop in her rent was right there in black and white, along with the reminder that she was aware this was not a real engagement and did not constitute a promise of marriage.

Clearly he'd thought ahead somewhat, despite the fact that buying the building in the first place was a radical idea. Not to mention faking an engagement.

Had anyone said to her this morning that she'd even remotely be considering going along with Rad's plan, she would have said they'd lost touch with reality. Rad was everything she wanted to avoid in life. He was big and bossy and arrogant and powerful.

Sure, he had that Adrian Paul thing going for him, with his dark hair and brooding eyes, and that slash of a smile that changed his entire face. But she'd never been a sucker for the dark, brooding type before. She preferred intellectual, sensitive types who shared her love of books.

But in the end, the offer was too good for Serena to pass up. She'd been struggling to make ends meet since she'd opened her bookstore a year ago. She was no longer a child unable to defend herself from a commanding personality. She could handle Rad.

"So what do you say?" he prompted her.

"Okay." Her voice was deliberately brisk.

"You'll do it?"

"Yes. But I have to warn you that things may get more complicated than you anticipate."

"Why? Is there some guy in your life who will be upset that you're engaged?"

Serena shook her head. She hadn't had the time or energy to date much since opening the store. The few men she had gone out with hadn't impressed her enough to see them for more than a few dates.

"Lies have a way of coming back to haunt you," Serena told him. She should know. There were things in her past that she feared would one day catch up with her.

Watching the way she nervously nibbled on her bottom lip made Rad wonder two things. First, what personal knowledge did she have about lies in her past? Second, how would her lips feel beneath his? Okay, so maybe he thought about that first, but he did take a moment to think about what she'd said before getting caught up in a fantasy about her mouth.

He'd noticed her lush lips the moment he'd first met her. And her legs. He couldn't see much of them today, as she was wearing a dress that swirled around her ankles. The thin material did have a nice way of clinging to her curves, however.

As for lying, well…Rad looked on this operation as more of a dark ops mission. Subterfuge and deception were requirements for a successful outcome, which in this case meant getting Heidi off his back.

Rad was confident that he could handle things. His sexual attraction to Serena was an added bonus. Not that he was looking to settle down and get married at this point in his life. That might be fine for his two older brothers but not for him. He valued his freedom.

But there was something to be said for hanging out with a gorgeous blond bookseller. Not that she was the kind of female who flaunted her good looks. No, she seemed to take care to keep them under wraps, like that ankle-length dress of hers. Which just made him want to unwrap her all the more.

She intrigued him. Made him want to learn more about her. Because there was a lot going on beneath her cool surface. When he'd touched her, the heat had been immediate. He'd always been good at intel and recon work. He looked forward to doing a little of both on her.

That wasn't all he wanted to do with her. He wanted to know if her lips tasted as lush as they looked. He wanted to feel her long legs wrapped around his bare hips….

Chill out, he ordered his throbbing body. She's just

a female. Enjoy the moment, but don't go looking for complications here.

He got out his PDA and got to work. "There are a few details we should get straight. Like how we met, how long we've known each other, that sort of thing. Then there's the ring. What's your ring size?"

"Seven. You're not going to buy a ring, are you?"

"You have something else in mind?"

"I could pick up something inexpensive, a CZ, at one of the discount stores."

"CZ?"

"Cubic Zirconia. Only a jeweler would be able to tell it's not real, if I get something realistic carat-wise."

"Okay. I'll leave the ring to you. But I'll pay for it."

"Under fifty dollars. I don't want to be worrying about losing it or anything."

"How would you lose it? I thought you were supposed to wear an engagement ring all the time and not take it off."

"That's in a real engagement, which this isn't."

"Okay… But spend at least a hundred. I don't want people thinking I'm cheap." He used the stylus to change screens. "I made a checklist…."

"If you're that prepared, I would have thought you'd have come up with a better cover story for your fiancée than saying the name of the first woman that came to mind. What did you tell her about me?"

"That you were a bookseller."

"That's all?"

"I may have said that you used to be a swimsuit model," Rad couldn't resist teasing her.

"You *what?*"

"Just kidding."

"I should hope so. No one would believe I was a swimsuit model."

"Why not?"

"Because real women have curves and I'm a real woman."

His eyes strolled over her from head to toe. "I had noticed that."

"I have hips." She pointed to them as if he needed help locating them.

"Yeah, you do." He nodded approvingly.

"Swimsuit models never have real hips."

"I like females with hips. And long legs. And long blond hair and green eyes. In fact, there are a lot of things I like about you."

His comment made her feel as if she'd swallowed a goldfish. Not that she'd ever done that, but still...

She had this strange fluttery feeling of what...anticipation? Is that what this was? She anticipated the next *Harry Potter* book, but it didn't make her all funny inside.

Great. Now she knew what this was. It had just been a while since she'd experienced it, and never to this extreme. This was sexual attraction. This was her hormones leaping up and yelling yes, yes, yes, come to momma.

This was her inner-female responding to all that yummy male testosterone wrapped up in Rad's six-foot-plus body.

Serena firmly ordered her hormones to shut up. She could not afford to be ruled by sex here. She needed to be a savvy businesswoman. To be practical. To be Serena Serious. "You don't know me at all." There, that was a practical, factual statement, even if she had delivered it in a too-breathy voice. Since when had she started sounding like Marilyn Monroe at Kennedy's birthday party?

"But I want to get to know you," Rad murmured. "And I need to if we're going to pull this off. Tell me what I should know."

"That I don't think this is going to work," she muttered. Not if leaping hormones got in the way.

"Of course it will work. We just need to do some prep work. Winning any battle is predicated on good recon and accurate intel ahead of time. I know you're a bookseller, and the Realtor told me you've been here a year. That's all I know."

"I'll write you a brief bio tonight then you can enter it in your PDA."

He shut the hi-tech device down and turned his full attention to her. "Some things are unforgettable. Forget writing the bio. Have dinner with me instead and we can work out the details while we eat. I know a good seafood place down on the beach. Unless you have other plans?"

"I suppose it would be a good idea to get our stories straight." That was her practical side speaking.

"Affirmative."

There, that was his military voice. Not his bossy military voice, just the crisp tones. Crisp was good. She could handle crisp. She could even do crisp herself. "Okay, then."

It wasn't okay when she nearly tripped over the long skirt of her dress when he handed her into his car a few minutes later. You'd think she'd never gotten into a silver gray Corvette before.

And you'd be right. She'd never gotten into a Corvette of any color before. The men she tended to date drove sensible cars like four-door sedans. Buicks or Oldsmobiles. Not low-slung race cars.

She was surprised and pleased to discover that Rad didn't drive as if he were trying out for the Indy 500. He showed no sign of road rage when a car filled with teenagers cut him off or when an older driver pulled in front of him and barely went the speed limit.

Twenty minutes later, Serena was seated at a table with an ocean view and a huge plate loaded with fresh steamed shrimp. The place wasn't fancy. The tablecloths were red-checked oilcloth instead of white linen. But the food smelled heavenly and the view was great. White-topped waves tossed their frothy manes as they landed upon the smooth beach with rhythmic regularity.

"This is nice."

Rad nodded. "You've never been here before?"

Serena shook her head.

"You're not originally from around here, are you? No accent," he added.

"I'm from all over. Mostly east coast although we lived in Indianapolis for a year when I was eight."

"Are you an army brat? You said your dad had been out of the military for a while now."

"He left the army when I was ten." Her crisp tone of voice made it clear that she didn't welcome any further discussion on that topic.

"What made you decide to settle here?"

"My best friend lives here. We were college roommates our freshman year at UNCW, the University of North Carolina at Wilmington. I came to visit her for her wedding several years ago and liked the area. I'm an ocean person, so I like being on the coast."

"I know what you mean. My older brother Striker has a beach house out on Pirate's Cove. It's a little island off the coast. I get over there as often as I can when he's not using the place. Since he's moved to San Antonio, it's vacant a lot of the time."

"Is he a Marine as well?"

"He's in the reserves. Most of his time these days is spent running King Oil and chasing after his baby son. He's as smart as a tree full of owls, to quote my Texan brother."

"Did you grow up in Texas?"

"No, although I did spend a summer or two there. Like you I grew up all over. My dad was a Marine, he's retired now. All my other brothers are Marines."

"All? How many are there?"

"My momma had five sons. The youngest two are twins."

"Are you the second oldest?"

"No, that honor goes to my brother Ben. I'm the middle child."

"Which means, if I remember my birth order character traits correctly, that you're the peacemaker in the family."

"Negative. That role falls to Ben. What about you? Do you have any brothers or sisters?"

"No. I'm an only child."

"Which means you're a high achiever and expect a lot from life." At her surprised look, Rad added, "Hey, I've read some of that birth order stuff, too. As an adult, only children tend to have high self-esteem."

She laughed and shook her head. "Not me."

"Why not?"

"My dad didn't want me getting a big head." Her tone was mocking but she could feel the muscles in her neck tensing up.

"Sounds like he gave you a hard time."

"You could say that."

"Did he hit you? Beat you?"

Not with his fists but with his words. But she couldn't say that because her throat closed and her mouth went dry.

She reached for her iced tea. The condensed moisture made the glass slippery and she almost lost her hold on it. The ice cubes clattering against the sides sounded unnaturally loud in the sudden silence.

"Steady there." Rad reached over to straighten the glass and set it back on the table. His fingers brushed against hers.

Had he tried to capture her hand in his, she would have snatched it away. Instead he gently rubbed his thumb against the back of her hand.

Serena frantically tried to come up with something sophisticated and funny to say, but was so distracted by her awareness of him and her turbulent emotions that all she could come up with was, "I don't like talking about my childhood."

Right. That was an understatement. Brilliant, Serena. She pulled her hand away, exiling it to her lap where her fingertips continued to hum from his touch.

"Then we'll talk about something else. Like how we met."

She frowned. "We met at the school two days ago."

"Where you were madder than a rained-on rooster."

She lifted an eyebrow at him. "Another of your Texan brother's quotes?"

"Actually that was one of my grandfather's."

"Yes, well, if I was aggravated with you, I had good reason."

"So you told me at the time. But we obviously can't use the truth in this case about how we met, so we need to come up with something else. How about you saw me and fell instantly in love with me?"

"How about you saw *me* and fell instantly in love with *me*," she instantly countered.

His slow smile was worth the wait. "That'll work too."

Okay, there went her hormones again. Time to haul out the common sense practical stuff. "I think we should just go with something vague, like we met through a mutual friend."

"That sounds boring."

"Boring is good." Hormones are bad. Bad hormones. Behave.

"Marines are not into boring."

"Fine," she retorted. "Then *you* think of something."

"Hmmm…"

She noticed the outer corner of Rad's eyes got all crinkly when he was thinking.

"My brother Striker met his wife when they had to work together," he continued. "And my brother Ben met his wife through her brother."

"Neither scenario would work in our case. I'm telling you, we should go with mutual friends. It's the simplest thing."

"I suppose you're right."

Did he really have to sound so doubtful when he said that? "And how did you romantically propose to me?" she asked. "Did you get down on bended knee?"

"How about the beach?" He nodded at the view out the window where the surf washed in. "I proposed to you on the beach at sunset."

"Only one problem with that. From here, the sun *rises* over the Atlantic ocean, it doesn't set over it. See, it's details like those that are going to get us in trouble."

He raised a dark eyebrow. "You'd rather I proposed to you at sunrise?"

"No." She refused to allow her heart to beat a little faster at the thought of him really proposing. She'd regained control of her wild inner-female self and she planned on keeping her locked up indefinitely. Serena Serious was in charge now. "We'll stick to your proposing on the beach. We don't have to say when."

"Heidi is gonna want to know the juicy details."

"Who says we have to tell her?"

"I do. Or she'll get suspicious. So here's the story. We met through mutual friends and I proposed on the beach here on Topsail Island while the sun set over the sound, not the ocean. You're an only child, you went to UNCW and got your degree in…?"

"Business administration," Serena replied.

"Before opening your own bookstore, you worked at…?"

"Various jobs, including the district manager of a large bookstore chain."

"You moved here to coastal North Carolina…?"

"Two years ago. Before that I lived in Raleigh, and

before that I was in the Boston area, and Virginia Beach before that."

Rad continued his questions through dessert and the drive home. It wasn't until Serena walked into her apartment later that evening that she realized that while she'd practically supplied him with her résumé, and even confessed her love of dark Belgian chocolate, Rad hadn't told her anything about what he did in the Marine Corps. Other than the little he'd told her about his family, he hadn't said much about himself at all.

That's when she remembered another trait of middle children. They can be secretive.

Chapter Three

"You what!"

Serena winced at her best friend's shriek and held the phone away from her ear for a second. Needing someone to talk to, Serena had curled up on her couch and called Lucy as soon as she'd stepped inside her apartment. She returned the receiver to her ear in time to hear Lucy say, "Start over again."

"The Marine who came to Becky's school's Career Day bought my building. And I'm engaged to him."

"To Bossy Marine Man who scared my little girl?"

"Yeah." Serena's voice sounded freaked even to her own ears.

"Is he there right now?"

"No."

"Then get out the Pistachio Pistachio ice cream, I'm comin' right over."

"Thanks, Lulu." Serena used the nickname she reserved for special occasions, and this one sure qualified.

She and Lucy had become friends as freshman college roommates at UNCW. Lucy had gotten pregnant and married after that first year, but she and Serena had remained very close.

By the time Serena cleared the junk mail from her pine dining table and got the ice cream out of the freezer and the bowls out of the cabinet, Lucy was knocking on her door.

The first thing she did was put her hand on Serena's forehead. "You don't feel like you're running a high fever."

"I'm not."

"If you're not delirious with a high fever then why would you say you were engaged to Bossy Marine Man?"

"His name is Rad Kozlowski."

"That doesn't sound like a Marine name to me. The Marines I know have solid, tough American names like Harry or Bud."

"His name is the least of my worries." Serena dug the red plastic scooper into the ice cream and dumped a sizable portion into Lucy's dish and then another huge scoop into her own.

"What did he do to you?"

"He bought my building and then offered to cut my rent in half if I'd help him."

"The rat buzzard. What did he want you to do? As if I couldn't guess."

Serena withdrew the spoon she'd just offered Lucy. "Before I tell you anything else, you have to swear you won't leak a word of this to anyone."

"I swear."

"Not even your husband." Serena waved the flatware for extra emphasis.

"What if we need him to beat up your Marine?"

Lucy's husband Alec was built like a linebacker, because he was one. He'd played that position in college. "We don't need Alec to beat up anyone. Now swear, on this carton of Pistachio Pistachio, that you won't tell a soul what I'm confiding in you."

Lucy solemnly placed her hand over the Ben & Jerry logo. "I swear. Now tell me what the rat buzzard wants you to do. Wait, let me eat a bite of ice cream first...."

Serena quickly did the same.

"Okay," Lucy mumbled around the cold dessert. "Tell me."

"He wants me to pretend to be his fiancée."

Lucy frowned. "Is he gay?"

"Thank you."

"For what?"

"For thinking the way I do. I thought that was his reason for asking me and he acted like I was crazy instead of it being a reasonable possibility."

"So is he?"

"No."

"You're sure?"

"Oh *yeah*."

"That's a very emphatic reply. Care to tell me how you can be so sure?"

"He almost kissed me. This is definitely a guy who likes women. Which is the problem. It seems there's a general's daughter who's been chasing him, and—"

"He's using a fiancée as an excuse to get rid of her."

"Something like that, yes."

"Why you?"

"My name just happened to slip out because the girl confronted him right after I met him at the school and we had a run-in."

"You didn't tell me you had a run-in with him."

After taking a huge bite, Serena dabbed at her chin with a paper napkin. "I didn't think it was worth mentioning."

"Clearly it made an impression on him—*you* made an impression on him if your name was the first that came to his mind."

"Do you think I'm really stupid to go along with this?"

"You haven't told me much about what 'this' actually is."

"Pretending to be his fiancée."

"For how long?"

"As long as it takes for her to lose interest. Look." She waved the contract at Lucy. "He even had this drawn up so I would be assured that my rent would be reduced, both for the store and the apartment. It's all here in writing." She jabbed the document with her index finger and broke her nail in the process.

Lucy took the paper from her and looked it over. "It also says that this is not a real engagement and does not constitute a proposal of marriage. I'd say the guy was commitment shy."

"He has nothing to worry about from me in that department."

"Because you're commitment shy too."

"With good reason."

"Maybe."

"Maybe?"

"Yeah, maybe. You don't really give most guys a chance to screw up. You dump them before they dump you."

"It's safer that way."

"Not all guys are like your father."

"Most aren't sweet like your Alec."

"Yet here you are engaged to a bossy military man, your worst nightmare."

"Yes, but I'm not *really* engaged. This is just a simple business arrangement."

"It's a lie. And you better than anyone should know how messy things can get as a result of a lie."

"I don't want to talk about that now." Serena was upset enough with the present situation. She really couldn't emotionally afford to dig up her past mistakes at the moment.

"Okay. I'm just saying that things can get complicated."

"I realize that. But I couldn't pass this up. The economic reality is that I need this decrease in the rent. Things have been tough."

"You haven't said anything."

"Because I don't like focusing on the negative."

"Yeah, you're just Serena Sunshine."

Serena stuck her tongue out at her.

Lucy grinned. "Well, you are. You always try to find the good in any situation."

"That didn't always come naturally for me. Quite the opposite. But I've made a concerted effort to learn to look for the silver lining."

"Well, you've been successful at it. Except where it applies to guys."

"Hey, I've dated several men recently, but none of them really made that big an impression."

"Because you tend to go for the bland, bookish types." Lucy brandished her empty spoon at Serena as a reprimand.

"Well, I sure don't usually go for the dark, brooding Adrian Paul type."

"Aha, so Bossy Marine Man is a hunk, huh?"

"He's good-looking in a big, broad-shouldered, sexy-gleam-of-humor-in-his-eyes kind of way."

"I thought you said he was the dark and brooding type."

"He is. Then he'll get this gleam of humor in his eyes and they kind of light up…" Serena paused as a vision of Rad's face filled her mind.

"Uh-oh."

"Uh-oh what?"

"Your cat is eating your ice cream."

"Bella, you little squirt!" Serena picked up the sleek, small gray cat and set her on the floor. "Now you know why I call her Bella-That's-Mine. She thinks everything in this house is hers. Oshi would never dream of stealing my ice cream." Serena had found the mother cat and her tiny kitten hidden near the Dumpster behind her building. She'd managed to coax the mom inside once she had the kitten in her hands. To her surprise, Oshi had taken one look around the apartment, walking around the perimeter to check things out, and then curled up on Serena's favorite area rug and started nursing.

Serena had had the two of them for almost a year now, and had gotten both the mom and her kitten spayed. The two of them provided Serena with some much-needed company and plenty of laughs.

Bella licked her chops, her pink tongue swirling over her black whiskers, before jumping onto Serena's lap where she curled up and started washing herself.

"Just be careful that you don't fall for this guy. I know how you are about strays." Lucy pointed at Bella. "Look at that cat. Living in the lap of luxury."

"Rad isn't a stray. He's a completely self-sufficient Marine."

"If he were that self-sufficient he wouldn't have needed your help, now would he?"

"Everyone needs a little help now and then."

"Help him and then get out."

"That's the plan."

"Good. Just be sure you stick to the plan."

The next morning Serena tried to focus on the fact that her rent was cut in half for the next year and not the fact that she'd agreed to pretend to be Rad's fiancée for an indefinite period of time.

Focus on the positive. And stay away from the chocolate. After Lucy had left, Serena had eaten half-a-dozen dark chocolate lemon-cream truffles from her hidden cache in the Shakespeare cookie jar. But then it wasn't every day that a girl got engaged, even if it wasn't for real.

The young woman walking into The Reader's Place in the low-riding jeans and skimpy designer T-shirt was for real, however. And she was looking around with the kind of dismissive attitude that immediately put Serena on edge.

Reminding herself that she was good with people, Serena was about to ask if she could help the woman when she spoke first.

"Does Serena Anderson work here?"

"I'm Serena Anderson."

Instead of introducing herself, the woman frowned at Serena's simple denim dress and sandals as if she were a fashion dinosaur.

"And you are?" Serena prompted her before reminding herself that getting aggravated with someone because they were younger, prettier and skinnier than you was not a good thing.

"My name is Heidi Burns. My father is General Burns."

Yeah, I was afraid of that. "Hi, Heidi. Rad told me about you."

Her face lit up. "Like seriously? He did? What did he say?"

Serena couldn't tell the truth of course. "Just that you know about our engagement."

"It's kind of sudden, isn't it?"

Serena just shrugged. It gave her a moment to collect her thoughts. She hadn't expected Heidi to show up so quickly. When had she and Rad said they'd met? Her mind suddenly went blank. Why hadn't she taken notes during their dinner last night?

"You're not wearing a ring."

"It's being sized." Serena had planned on stopping by a few stores later that afternoon to find something reasonable.

"So how did you two like meet?"

"Through a mutual friend." That was right, wasn't it?

Wasn't that what they'd finally decided? After the falling in love at first sight nonsense?

"A mutual friend?"

Serena nodded. Surely there had to be some advantage in being older than Heidi? Wasn't she supposed to have more confidence and stuff like that?

Why, oh why had she eaten that carton of ice cream last night? And the chocolate.

Heidi probably never ate ice cream. She nibbled on lettuce to fit into those size zero jeans.

Or maybe, even worse, Heidi was one of those horrible people with a fast metabolism who could eat like a horse and never gain a pound. If that was the case, then Serena granted herself permission to really dislike Heidi.

At least Serena was taller than Heidi. Big deal. Guys didn't lust after gawky giraffes, they went for the petite little things with big breasts.

And okay, yeah, Serena could hold her own in the bra-cup division—without any artificial assistance from implants or water bras, thank you very much. But her big breasts were matched with a big bottom. And while Jennifer Lopez might make that look appealing, the star was much tinier than Serena.

Okay, stop it. You cannot have a self-image meltdown in front of this girl. Healthy women have curves. You're a healthy women with lots of curves. So stop with the criticism, Serena ordered herself.

"Who?"

"Who what?" Serena had lost track of the conversation, engrossed as she'd been in her own self-discussion bouncing around in her head.

"Who's this mutual friend that introduced you to Rad?"

"No one you'd know."

"How do you know that?"

Serena decided it was time to take control of things here and turn the tables on Heidi. "I'm honored that you'd come all the way out here to my bookstore just to meet me. You must care about Rad a lot."

"Rad and I have like a very, very special connection." Heidi's smile indicated that that connection had been an intimate one.

All I did was smile at her. Serena replayed Rad's words in her head. Had he lied to her? Was he faking this engagement to get off the hook after having an affair with the general's daughter? If that was the case, Serena didn't want any part of this—discounted rent or not.

But a closer look at Heidi revealed the fact that the younger woman couldn't seem to maintain eye contact with Serena. Of course that could mean that Heidi was lying. Or it could just mean that Heidi was offended by what she clearly perceived to be Serena's utter lack of fashion sense.

"He's like never mentioned anything about you before yesterday." Heidi obviously took great pleasure in pointing out that fact. And this time she met Serena's gaze head on. Okay, so she was telling the truth with that statement.

"I'm not surprised that he didn't mention me to you," Serena replied.

"Why not?"

"Because Rad's not the kind to go around talking about his private life with other people."

Heidi's frown indicated her displeasure over being lumped in with "other people."

"You are so *not* his type."

"What is his type?" Okay, so she was only human and the question slipped out before Serena could stop it.

"Brunettes with blue eyes and great bodies."

Hah. Heidi had just described herself.

"Feminine girls," Heidi added. "Not nerdy types who work in a bookstore."

"I don't just work here, I happen to own this bookstore."

Heidi shrugged as if that fact were irrelevant.

Don't let her get to you. Ignore the fact that she's a petite size zero and you struggle to stay a size ten. Okay, a size twelve.

"I'm going to own my own business someday," Heidi announced.

"Really? What kind of business?"

"I don't know. Like, I haven't decided that part yet. Something more exciting than a bookstore."

"Naturally."

"People don't always take me seriously just like…just because I'm like beautiful. That doesn't mean I'm dumb."

"Of course not." Shallow maybe. Not necessarily dumb.

"I'm a very ambitious person."

"I'm sure you are."

They were interrupted by the arrival of Clay Twitty entering the bookstore. It was only then that Serena realized that a customer could have overheard her conversation with Heidi. Then she had to remind herself that she hadn't actually said anything unkind to Heidi, she'd just thought it.

"Hello, Clay." Serena smiled at him, glad for a break.

Clay was her computer expert. Occasionally he helped out in the store, but his field of expertise was maintaining the store's Web site. He'd just started his freshman year at the local community college. With his pale skin, freckles and red hair, Clay was your typical nerd.

But he was also a male, which meant that his tongue was just about hanging out as he gazed at Heidi in silent adoration.

The object of his desire appeared accustomed to such things and gave no indication that she even noticed Clay after initially dismissing him. "Rad and I have that in common," Heidi continued as if Clay weren't there. "We're both ambitious. We have so much in common. Outsiders can't understand military life."

"My father was in the military."

Heidi gave her another one of those demeaning I-am-so-much-more-fabulous-than-you-are looks. "Enlisted? Army?"

The girl had ESP. The evil side of Serena wanted to lie and say no, her father was Chairman of the Joint Chiefs of Staff in the White House. That same evil side wanted to bury the general's daughter under a pile of *Harry Potter* books. The weight alone would squash Heidi. What chance did a size zero have against a nine-hundred page tome? Just one or two books would probably do the trick.

"That doesn't mean you could like understand what Rad and I share," Heidi continued. "The Marine Corps is different. When you get to know Rad, I think you'll understand like how things are."

"I already understand how things are, Heidi."

Uh-oh. Heidi frowned at her suspiciously. "What do you mean?"

"Just that Rad is my fiancé." *Not that he told me you're chasing him and he only got engaged to me to fend you off.*

"Whatever." Heidi was clearly not completely convinced.

Great. Serena could see that she was going to have to work hard to earn her discounted rent. But then she should know better than most that lying was never as easy as it seemed.

"Do you need help finding a book?" Clay's face was almost as red as his hair as he finally screwed up the courage to approach Heidi.

"Like I'd have time to read?" Her attitude made it clear that pretty girls like her weren't losers like him.

Okay, it was one thing to be rude to her, but no one demeaned Serena's employees. "Heidi was just leaving," Serena told Clay with a warm smile in his direction. She even held the door open for her.

Heidi took the hint. "I just came to look at you," she told Serena as she moseyed past her.

Serena bit her tongue and stopped herself from doing anything she'd regret later. But it was hard. Harder than she'd expected when Rad had first talked her into this stupid plan of his.

Rad had an unexpected visitor of his own to cope with. Wanda Kozlowski, Rad's Polish grandmother, his *Busha*, from Chicago had arrived in North Carolina for an extended stay with Rad's brother Ben and his family. Ben had promised her a tour of the base, but then had been called away so he'd dropped their *Busha* off with Rad to finish the tour.

It never failed to amaze Rad how petite his *Busha* was. Despite barely reahing five feet, she had a huge personality, filling the space around her with intelligence, humor, and caring. She had the bluest eyes he'd ever seen and a smile that lit her entire face. Never one to conform to fashion, she wore bright red pants and a colorful T-shirt that said Age Is Mind Over Matter. If You Don't Mind, It Doesn't Matter.

Rad leaned way down as she engulfed him in her hug. *Busha* was never one to do things half-way. She'd always been a toucher, patting the hands of complete strangers. "You look well, *Busha*."

"I looked better fifty years ago. You should have seen me then."

"I've seen the photos. I can see why Grandpa fell for you the instant he saw you."

"I was only seventeen when the war ended. My parents smuggled me out when the Nazis invaded Poland. They died shortly after." Her blue eyes became shadowed with sad memories.

Rad saw his grandmother's pain and wished there was something he could do about it. But he'd never been good at handling emotions.

In the Marine Corps he was trained to respond with action. You ditched emotions and just did your job.

Rad knew he was a damned good Marine. His ranking in the grandson department was another matter.

Wanda took a deep breath and continued her story. "I was in England during the war not knowing the language much. That's where I ran into your grandfather.

He was a dashing American soldier named Kozlowski, in his early twenties. He spoke my language and we conversed in Polish. We were married within two weeks of first meeting. He brought me back to Chicago with him. I knew little English, but with so many people from my homeland living in our neighborhood, I felt right at home. Chicago has the largest collection of Poles outside of Warsaw, you know."

Rad nodded.

"Eventually I did learn English, of course. And I had children. Your father and your two uncles."

"And dad became a Marine and met a girl and married her." Rad gave his own thumbnail version.

"Your mother was not just a girl. She was the daughter of a wealthy Texas oilman who did not approve of her marrying a penniless Kozlowski from Chicago. Her father threatened to disown her if she wed my son."

"You never met Hank King did you?"

Wanda shook her head. "And now he is gone. Like my beloved Chuck. And despite the threats of disowning your mother, Hank King's money has now come to her and her sons."

"Thanks to Striker. If he hadn't obeyed the terms of the will and gone to Texas to take over the helm at King Oil, the entire thing would have gone under. Not that Striker or any of us wanted the money."

"It would have come in useful all those years your father and mother were struggling."

Rad nodded his agreement. "Well, at least they're doing okay now."

"They certainly are. They are touring New England in the RV, looking at the fall colors. I got a call from them just yesterday from Vermont. I told them to get me some maple syrup. You don't have maple syrup down here in North Carolina do you?"

"Sure we do. In the supermarket."

"Oh, you!" She affectionately socked his arm.

"Are you ready for your tour of the base now?"

"First tell me what you do here."

"I save the world from evil."

"Oh, you!" She socked his arm again. "I can never tell when you are kidding and when you are not." She studied him as if just noticing his uniform. "I like your dress blues uniform better than this green one. You and all your brothers all look so handsome in those dress blues."

"I so totally agree." Rad didn't have to turn around to identify the female voice as belonging to Heidi. "I don't know about his brothers, but Rad is like totally hot."

"You know this young girl, Rad?"

Before he could reply, Heidi said, "I'm only a few years younger than Rad."

A few years? She was light years younger than he was. "She's the general's daughter and her name is Heidi Burns. If you'll excuse us, Heidi, I was just about to give my grandmother a tour of the base."

Rad should have known by the look in Heidi's eyes that she was up to something. Even so, he didn't see this particular salvo coming in time. "Don't you want to hear about my visit with your fiancée?"

"Fiancée?" Wanda was clearly stunned as she drew herself up to her full four-foot-eleven-inch height and glared at Rad in disbelief. "What is this about a fiancée?"

Chapter Four

Rad had never seen a general's daughter smirk before. It was not a pretty picture.

Heidi batted her eyelashes at him. "Rad, I can't believe that you haven't like told your grandmother about your engagement."

He immediately went into damage control mode. "She just got here," he said, then wondered why he'd even bothered given the way Heidi rolled her eyes in the universal way that women had, no matter what their age. He'd even caught his six-year-old niece Amy doing it when his brother Ben had told her that no, they couldn't buy a miniature golf course and rebuild it in their backyard.

"Even so, I would think that's like something you'd let her know about right away." Heidi shared a commiserative look with his grandmother, one that said, *I share your pain. Men can be so dense sometimes.*

Wanda turned her head and frowned at him, her light blue eyes laser sharp. When he'd been a little kid, four or something, Rad had been convinced that she could read his thoughts just by giving him that I-know-what-you're-up-to-so-you-might-as-well-tell-me-now look. "Rad, you are engaged?"

He nodded. He hated lying to his grandmother, but there was nothing he could do about it now. Not without sabotaging his mission of getting Heidi off his back.

"Is she Polish?" Wanda demanded. "What is her name?"

"Her name is Serena Anderson," Rad replied.

Wanda appeared disappointed. "That is not a Polish name."

"My mother was one-half Polish." Heidi smiled at Wanda.

Rad saw the way his grandmother focused her attention on the general's daughter, as if considering her as a possible candidate for *Busha*'s matchmaking skills.

He was no fool. He could see where this was going. Heidi was like the evil serpent trying to lure his poor grandmother closer. He had to get his *Busha* away…before she tried to hook him up with Heidi.

"Actually Serena's mother is *three-quarters* Polish," he fabricated desperately. "Excuse us, Heidi, but we're on our way to see her now."

"You just said you were taking your grandmother on a tour of the base," Heidi reminded him.

"That was before I realized what time it is. We have to hurry or we'll be late."

Taking his grandmother's arm, he hustled her toward the parking lot and his waiting Corvette.

"That one has her eyes on you," Wanda said, "and I think she is a young woman used to getting her own way."

"The general's daughter is definitely used to getting her own way."

He helped his grandmother into the low-slung passenger seat. "This is not a car for old people," she grumbled.

"You're not old, *Busha*."

"I cannot believe you did not tell me of your engagement, Radoslaw." Her use of his full name indicated her displeasure. Most of his buddies assumed that he was called Rad because of his radical ways, which was exactly the way he liked it. He could only be thankful that his grandmother hadn't used his full name in front of Heidi.

"I can't believe the entire situation," Rad muttered. He could feel the muscles at the back of his neck tightening as he turned his head to back his Corvette out of its parking space. This car was his pride and joy. The automotive work of art had a bodacious swagger that proclaimed its power and speed to all who shared streetspace with it.

The first thing he'd done when he'd received his inheritance from his oil tycoon grandfather was get this car. The second was to make a generous donation to the Make-A-Wish Foundation.

"Do not drive too fast," his grandmother cautioned him, grabbing on to the dashboard as he turned a corner. "I am eager to meet your fiancée, but I do not want to risk my life to do so."

Rad had never intended for his family to know about his elaborate deception. But now, thanks to Heidi, he had to take his grandmother to the bookstore to meet Serena.

Fine. Change of plans. He could handle that. He'd been trained to manage multiple scenarios with various outcomes. Dealing with rapidly changing conditions was his specialty. Answering the barrage of questions about Serena that his grandmother threw at him was not.

He decided not to mention that he'd just bought Serena's building. Instead he just nodded when his grandmother commented on the lovely flower boxes at the front windows of the store.

Wanda touched a fingertip to one of the red petunias as if she could gain critical information from its petals. "So this Serena of yours, she is a good girl, yes?"

"Affirmative."

Rad held the door open for his grandmother and walked into the bookstore to find Serena on a ladder, hanging a huge banner. Distracted as he was by her legs—her trim ankles, her curvaceous calves, the vulnerable backs of her knees, the sexy smoothness of her thighs— it took him a moment or two to realize what was actually printed on that banner. It said Welcome Sexual Goddess!

The cozy bookstore he remembered from yesterday had been transformed. Posters on easels displayed suggestive book covers and a photo of a blond woman with a plastic smile and a lot of cleavage, nowhere near as good as Serena's cleavage but still…. Piles of books with provocative titles like *Sexual Satisfaction* in big letters were stacked all around them.

"What are you doing?" His Marine voice boomed out.

Startled, Serena glanced over her shoulder and ended up swaying dangerously on the ladder and almost falling off. Rad caught her before that happened and then momentarily held her in his arms as if unsure what to do with her.

Which was ridiculous. He knew exactly what to do with her. Or what he *wanted* to do with her. He wanted those long sexy legs of hers around his waist....

His grandmother tugged on his sleeve. "You can put her down now."

He couldn't dump Serena fast enough.

Serena blinked as Rad set her on her feet with all the finesse of a longshoreman and then glared at her as if she were running a house of ill repute. The older woman at his side looked around with unabashed interest.

What now, Serena wondered. This was Rad's charade, so she waited to let him speak first.

But he was too busy giving her the evil eye. So naturally she had to leap into the conversational void, feeling the need to explain the display she'd just finished putting up. "A very well-known sex therapist and bestselling author is coming here tomorrow for a book signing. She's known as the Sexual Goddess."

"And here I thought you were welcoming me," Wanda said with a huge grin.

Rad's square jaw dropped, a rare occurrence for a man who prided himself on maintaining the upper hand at all times. "Aren't you going to introduce me to your fiancée?" his grandmother demanded, poking him with her finger as she'd done back in her kitchen in Chicago when he'd tried to steal a *kolachki* from the cookie sheet right out of the oven.

Rad still hadn't recovered from being caught red-handed with Serena in his arms and X-rated thoughts in his mind. He'd definitely known his share of women, but he'd never had his grandmother standing by on the sidelines while he'd engaged in his sexual pursuits.

Okay, he was just momentarily thrown. No problem. He'd regroup and regain control. "Serena, this is my grandmother Wanda Kozlowski. She's down here for an unexpected visit."

"Unexpected by you maybe," Wanda said. "But your brother Ben knew I was coming." Without waiting for Rad to continue, she went over to Serena and enfolded her in a huge hug. "And you must be Serena Anderson. I had no idea Rad got engaged until his friend Heidi told me."

Rad said, "I was going to surprise my grandmother, but that's no longer possible thanks to Heidi."

"I'm sure you will continue to do things to surprise your grandmother. I know you are always doing things to surprise me." Serena shot him a look that said, *Duping little old ladies wasn't part of the deal*.

"My Rad tells me that your mother is three-quarters Polish. What part of Poland did her family come from?"

Behind Wanda's back, Rad's hand gesture was the all-too-familiar one for go along with whatever I say.

Serena did her best to keep up. "Uh, I'm not sure."

"Do your parents live nearby?"

"No way."

Serena's emphatic reply raised a few eyebrows in the Kozlowski family.

"I mean, no. They live way on the other side of the country. In Las Vegas."

"Rad has told me very little about you. He didn't go into detail about your Polish relatives. He only said that your mother is three-quarters Polish, but had little more information than that. You know how men are. They do not notice the small things. Not that your Polish heritage is a small thing."

"Of course not."

"So tell me more." Wanda gave her an encouraging smile.

"I really don't know much more than that."

"Your mother shared none of her Polish heritage with you? What about Dyngus Day? It is the day after Easter and a holiday in Poland."

"No, I'm sorry."

"The contributions which Poles have made to science, music, art and literature are outstanding. Think of the beautiful music of Chopin, or the scientific contributions of Marie Curie, to name just two of many. Ours is a proud heritage. I am sorry for what you have missed."

Serena had missed more than that in her childhood. In reality, she had no idea about her parents' backgrounds, other than the fact that her mother's parents were strict Baptists and her father was overly strict period.

No, it wasn't lack of knowledge about her heritage that she'd missed, it had been acceptance and understanding.

"Do not look so sad." Wanda patted her cheek. "I can tell you more about your Polish heritage. I would be glad to do so."

Serena felt like pond scum for deceiving her.

"But you are not wearing a ring." Wanda held up Serena's left hand to show Rad. "Why is she not wearing a ring?" she asked him.

"It's being sized," Serena replied.

"Had I known of Rad's intentions, I would have offered my own engagement ring for your use. But this one tells me nothing." She affectionately socked Rad's arm before returning her attention to Serena. "You and I must get to know one another better without his help."

"Serena is going to be very busy with her bookstore." Rad's voice was firm.

"You are so young to own such a business. You must work very hard." She turned from Serena to gaze at her grandson in exasperation. "And you, you can stop glaring at that sign. This is not the first time I have heard of the Sexual Goddess. I read her first book."

His jaw dropped for the second time. "You did?"

"Of course. Why do you think your grandfather died with a smile on his face? Ah, it is so easy to shock these young ones." Wanda laughed, a super-sized sound coming from such a petite woman. "Now you must tell me how you two met. Did Rad come to your store for a book?"

Behind his grandmother's back, Rad was once again indicating to Serena that she should along with whatever he was about to say.

Serena couldn't help but be amused by Rad's flustered behavior. Having seen him in his "U.S. Marine mode" she knew how in command and supremely confident he was most of the time. Because it felt good to be able to throw him off balance for a change, she said, "Actually he came in to buy the Sexual Goddess's latest book."

Wanda laughed, the sound once again filling the bookstore.

"She's kidding." Rad's look promised retribution later.

"A sense of humor is a good thing." Wanda nodded her approval. "It will come in handy dealing with this one." She tilted her head toward Rad.

"I'm sure it will."

"How long have you been engaged? When did he pop the question?" The older woman's vivid blue eyes glowed with excitement and curiosity. "What did he say?"

"You know Rad. He made me an offer too good to refuse."

"Ah, he has a way with words. Not that he says much, but when he does, they mean something."

"He's an impressive speaker." She remembered the way he'd spoken at the school. "Sometimes I don't think he realizes the power in his own voice."

"That's the Marines. All my grandsons are like that. They all have a Marine's voice. My son as well."

Rad stepped closer, as if his doing so would allow him to regain control of the situation. "Dad says he got that from you, not from the Marines."

Wanda shrugged. "When you have children, you keep a certain voice reserved to let them know when you mean business. Discipline is never a problem then."

Serena's father had used that I-mean-business-so-don't-mess-with-me voice all the time, over everything—from what time meals should be served, to ordering her to dust the baseboards all around the house every Saturday morning, to ordering her out of his house. *Don't go there. Keep the past in the past.*

Wanda gazed fondly at her grandson. "Everyone

knows that I am really a marshmallow. Rad especially has always had a way of getting to me. He is always doing the unexpected. Remember the time you painted the kitchen walls with Crisco?"

"I was only two at the time."

"Four," Wanda corrected him. "And as full of the devil as anything. Ah, the pranks this one pulled. There were times I thought I would never live to see sixty-five for the wild things he did."

"And now you're seventy-five and doing just fine."

Wanda nodded. "That is true. So when are you two getting married? Have you set a date yet? I wasn't able to come to either of my other grandson's weddings. His brother Ben had two, you know. One was a quickie in a wedding chapel with only his parents present. You aren't planning on doing that are you?"

"Definitely not," Serena stated emphatically.

"Good. I missed Striker's Texas wedding because I'd just broken my ankle the day before. And I was having my gallbladder removed when Ben and Ellie renewed their vows a few months ago."

"Sounds like your grandsons' weddings bring you bad luck," Serena noted.

"It may sound that way," Wanda agreed, "but it isn't true. I am so happy to see them finally settle down. There were times when I was sure this one here would never do so. Not after Liza."

There was an awkward silence.

The shadowed look in Rad's eyes told her that this was confidential information, that only those with top clearance were allowed access to that part of his life. As a fake fiancée, she wasn't privy to his innermost feelings. And clearly he had had feelings for this Liza, who-ever she was. *Deep* feelings, judging by the way his jaw clenched and his expression tightened at the mere mention of her name.

Serena tried not to be hurt by this new knowledge. Who was the woman who'd managed to touch Rad's heart?

"But enough about that." Wanda said quickly.

"We really should get going." Rad's voice was curt. "Ben is expecting us."

"Serena must come with us. You should have invited her before," she scolded Rad before taking Serena's hands in hers once more. "You'll come, yes?"

Behind Wanda's back, Rad was shaking his head.

"It wouldn't be right for me to accept," Serena politely said. "I'm sure your family has plans for you tonight."

What she really wanted to know was who Liza was and why the mere mention of her name made Rad's expression freeze.

"The plan was for grilled hamburgers in Ben's backyard. Besides, no plans could be bigger than celebrating your engagement. Unless your brother already has met Serena and didn't tell me?" Wanda turned her eagle gaze onto Rad who shook his head. "Then it is time he met her now. And Ellie. You will like her and her daughter Amy," Wanda told Serena before chastising Rad. "What were you thinking, hiding your news and your lovely fiancée this way?"

"I was trying to keep her to myself for a little while," Rad said.

"Ah, he is such a romantic, this one."

The sight of the little Polish grandma patting the lean mean Marine's cheek was enough to make Serena smile. "Really? A romantic?"

"Oh, yes. And he's funny. You wouldn't think so to look at him now, standing there glaring at us. But I remember the time he ran naked out of my house...."

Rad groaned. "Do not tell that story."

"Ignore him." Serena tucked her arm through Wanda's. "Tell me more."

"There's no time." Rad firmly placed his arm around Serena and led her away from his grandmother. "Serena may want to go change for dinner."

"Go where?" Wanda asked.

"I live upstairs," Serena explained.

"You go ahead and get ready," Wanda said. "I'll just look around your store. I want to buy some books to read."

Serena nodded toward Kalinda, who'd been manning the register. "My assistant will take care of you. I won't be long."

Serena was slightly delayed by her kitties Oshi and Bella who demanded they get their fair share of petting before permitting her to get past them in the living room. Then they took off, chasing one another in their favorite game of tag, zooming down the hallway as if it were a Nascar racetrack.

As with the bookstore, Serena had put her own individual stamp on her apartment. She'd sewn the couch slipcovers—red with a skinny yellow piping—herself. The colorful throw pillows in a cheerful tropical fabric were another of her finds. She liked gregarious colors, bold splashes of red or fresh dashes of yellow and orange.

Her love of the ocean was apparent in the beach

theme painting she'd picked up at an art fair and in the blue-and-white decor of her tiny bathroom.

She shoved the striped shower curtain aside and turned on the water with one hand while kicking off her sandals. She twisted her hair into a knot and secured it with a banana clip. A second later she stood naked under the spray of lukewarm water. The building's hot water heater wasn't the best.

Even with its quirks, Serena loved her home. And she considered this apartment to be home. The high ceilings and elaborate architectural elements were a throwback to a different time, to the late 1930s when the building was built.

So what if the bathroom wasn't much bigger than a closet. It had all the necessities. Shower, sink, toilet. All worked, most of the time.

The silver linings far overshadowed any shortcomings. Tall windows in the living room let in plenty of sunlight. The yellow curtains she'd done up added to the airy look. And the kitchen wasn't too bad. Nothing big, but it suited her needs. As long as the freezer was large enough to hold a few cartons of ice cream, she was a happy camper.

Thinking of ice cream reminded her of Heidi's visit earlier in the day. She had a feeling that the general's daughter had not been totally convinced about Rad's engagement. Was it true that Serena wasn't Rad's usual type? Had Liza been?

Who was she? What had she been to Rad? And what had Liza done to make his expression turn so bleak?

Her thoughts were consumed with Rad and the mysterious Liza as Serena wrapped a towel around herself. Still tucking it in under her arms, she was looking down when she opened her bathroom door and ran into…a wall…a warm masculine wall of immovable force. Rad.

His hands on her bare arms steadied her, but nearly dislodged her towel. Grabbing it, she glared at him. "What are you doing in here?"

"Your front door was unlatched. Do you have any idea how dangerous that is? Anyone could have walked in."

Rad's presence in her state of undress unsettled Serena. So did the way her body responded to his closeness. So she called up her defenses. "I've been meaning to complain to the new landlord about fixing that door." Her voice was tart, not stupid and breathless. Good.

"Why did you agree to come to dinner?" Rad demanded, keeping his hands on her bare arms.

"Why didn't you tell me about your grandmother?" she countered, wanting to step away but afraid that doing so might dislodge her precarious hold on her bath towel.

"I was thinking I wouldn't have to let my family in on our charade."

"Well, apparently you thought wrong. Not for the first time, either."

"What's that supposed to mean?"

His obvious aggravation fired her own anger. "You thought pretending to be engaged to me would be a simple matter."

"And I thought you were going to help me out and make things easier," Rad growled. "Not more complicated."

One second he was glaring at her, and the next he was kissing her.

Chapter Five

Serena hung onto her towel for dear life. There was no use even trying to hang on to her composure. That had flown out the window the second his lips covered hers.

If Rad had kissed her with anger, Serena would have shoved him away without hesitation. But instead he devoured her with passion. There was no fighting that. Not when it felt so good. This was better than good. This was heaven. All consuming. His hands slid up her bare arms to her shoulders, his touch communicating strength, mastery and tenderness.

Not that he was subduing her. He was *seducing* her with every tantalizing thrust of his tongue. She'd parted her lips willingly and was now reveling in the increased pleasure of his mouth on hers. She was burning up inside. The heat of his kiss and his body was exhilarating.

There was no time for thought, no gradual escalation

in the intimacy of their first kiss. It had started out with devouring hunger and it continued on that way, on his part…and on hers. She gave as good as she got, matching his exploration with a boldness she never knew she possessed. Serena Sensuous, that was her.…

"Yoo-hoo. Rad, are you and Serena ready yet?"

The sound of Wanda's cheerful voice echoing up the hallway outside her apartment was enough to shatter Serena's momentary immersion in desire.

Gasping, she pulled away, barely hanging onto her bath towel. She stared at Rad with wide-eyed confusion.

He stared back with an unreadable expression in his dark eyes.

Leaving him to take care of Wanda, Serena hightailed it into her bedroom with a speed that would have done her cats proud. Once there, she shut the door and locked it, bouncing her derriere on the wood to make sure the door was totally latched.

What had just happened?

He kissed you, you idiot.

I know that. I've been kissed before. But not like that.

She should cancel, she should tell Rad she couldn't go visit his brother. She could tell Wanda she wasn't feeling well.

Her head was spinning and her fingers were trembling.

A sure sign of sexual attraction, but maybe it was the flu. She could tell Wanda she was coming down with the flu.

What was one more lie after so many?

No. Serena was not going to hide in her room like…like her mother. She was going to hold her head high and get the job done. And the job was pretending to be Rad's fiancée.

She hadn't considered the fact that kissing might be part of the package. Bad planning on her part. She should have thought ahead.

She could handle this. One step at a time. She dressed quickly. She would manage, just as she'd always managed in the past.

"I'm bringing someone." Rad spoke into his cell phone. He'd caught his grandmother before she'd come upstairs, assuring her that he'd be down shortly, and was now calling his brother from the hallway outside Serena's apartment.

"Yeah, I know," Ben replied. "*Busha* called me to come pick her up at some bookstore."

"Why did she do that?"

"Because your Corvette is a two-seater and if you're bringing someone that means there's no place for *Busha* to sit…unless you planned on strapping our grandmother to the roof of your car?"

"Very funny."

"So, you want to tell me what's up?"

"Not really, but I probably need to give you the latest intel on the situation."

"What situation?"

"I'm engaged."

"Come again?"

"You heard me."

"When did this happen?"

"Recently. She's the person I'm bringing tonight at *Busha's* insistence."

"Does this female have a name?

"Serena Anderson. She owns the bookstore where you're picking up *Busha*."

"Nice place."

"How do you know?"

"Because I just pulled up in front and *Busha* is coming out."

"Listen, whatever I say tonight just go along with it, understood? *Busha* knows nothing."

"She knows more than I do if she's already met your fiancée."

"Serena is a good girl," Rad could hear *Busha* saying in the background. "Her mother is three-quarters Polish but taught her nothing of her heritage."

Ben said, "I'm sure you'll fix that, right, *Busha*?"

"Remember, go along with whatever I say," Rad reminded Ben.

"Don't I always?" his older brother mocked him.

"Rarely."

"Who are you talking to?" *Busha* demanded.

"Rad."

"Tell him not to dillydally. I am going to make cheese pierogies tonight."

"You heard her." Rad could tell his brother was having a hard time not cracking up. "No dillydallying."

Rad's muttered curse relayed the fact that he did not appreciate his brother's humor.

"So does Striker know?" Ben asked.

"No."

"Mom and Dad?"

"No, and don't you even think about telling them."

"Hey, it's your funeral," Ben noted cheerfully.

"Yeah, it is."

"See you later, bro."

Rad turned around to find Serena standing behind him.

She'd exchanged her bath towel for a very respectable and in his opinion way-too-long black skirt. Her red sleeveless top looked like *Busha* could have knit it, but it did show off Serena's breasts even if it also covered them up. When he moved forward he was intrigued to see the slit in the skirt that revealed the curve of her knee and just a hint of thigh.

Her blond hair was piled on top of her head with a few loose strands falling around her face. She wore dangly silver earrings and a silver bracelet and watch. No rings.

He eyed her bare left finger. "We have to get an engagement ring tomorrow."

"I've got the book signing tomorrow."

"With the Sexual Goddess."

"That's right."

"We'll go after that. We have an agreement, remember."

"There's no way I could forget." There was no way she could forget the kiss they'd so recently shared either. Although Rad apparently was not suffering from the same difficulty. Judging by his attitude, he'd moved on. For a moment she thought he'd given her a heated look when he'd first seen her, but then he'd regained his war face, devoid of expression.

He was no doubt accustomed to kissing so many women that she was just one in a crowd. And while she'd kissed a fair number of men, she'd never experienced the jolt of raw pleasure she'd felt when his lips had covered hers.

Even now, just the memory of it was enough to set her heart racing.

Serena Sensuous needed locking up so that Serena Serious could come back out and regain control of the situation. "Tell me about the brother we're visiting tonight."

"Ben doesn't know the real story."

She lifted an eyebrow. "The real story being?"

"That this is a fake engagement."

"Fake" somehow sounded cheesier than make-believe or pretend engagement. She stifled the unexpected pang by focusing her attention on locking her apartment door. By the time she turned, she'd shoveled her emotions beneath a calm veneer. "Tell me which brother Ben is again."

"He's the second oldest." Rad shot her an impatient look while holding the downstairs door open for her. "Maybe you should be writing this down so you don't forget."

"Ben, the caretaker in the family. Married his wife Ellie a little over a year ago. She had a child named Amy that Ben has since adopted. Amy is six. Am I right so far?"

"Affirmative."

Two hours later, Serena knew even more. She'd discovered that Amy had asthma and loved a stuffed dragon named Ernie Infernie, based on stories Ben made up for her. And that Ben adored his new family. He also loved razzing his younger brother, who seemed to enjoy razzing him right back. There was a camaraderie there, that as an only child, Serena could only envy.

"They're something, aren't they?" Ellie noted fondly as she watched the two men jockeying for position in front of the state-of-the-art outside grill. "I have to confess that the first time I saw the brothers all together, I almost drowned in the ocean of testosterone."

"Ben's the first brother I've met." Serena took a sip of iced tea.

"He's the best one, but I may be prejudiced in saying that."

Serena shared a smile with Ellie, who then added, "I'm sure you think Rad is the best one."

"I'm sure the brothers are all special in their own way."

"They're all Marines, you know."

Serena nodded. "I know. Rad already told me."

"When he caught the garter at the renewal of our vows ceremony a few months ago, no one really believed that Rad would ever settle down."

"I can understand that." Men like Rad didn't marry brainy booksellers and settle down. They went with seductive sirens with exotic names like Giselle and had sex with them in the back seat of his Corvette.

Wait, his car didn't have a back seat.

Okay, then he had sex with them in other evocative places—against a wall in their apartment, perhaps.

"We think it's a good thing, though," Ellie stated.

What? Rad making love to the exotic Giselle was a good thing?

"He needed someone to give him roots."

If only Ellie knew the truth, that Serena was only a fake fiancée and that her own roots didn't go that deep. She'd moved around so much as a kid that she'd always longed for someplace permanent, a place you kept and didn't pack up and leave.

But that was the lifestyle of the military and therefore of their family as well. Just one of the many reasons why Serena shouldn't get romantically involved with Rad.

"Not that Rad doesn't take his responsibilities seriously," Ellie was saying. "And since I've only been married less than eighteen months myself, I'm probably not experienced enough to be giving you advice."

"Sure you are. If you've got any tips on how to deal with stubborn Marines, I'd be more than happy to hear them."

Ellie laughed. "You sound like me when I first met Ben. When he walked into the bar where I was working, I didn't want anything to do with him. He started giving me orders almost instantly. They can't seem to help themselves. Even now he reverts back sometimes."

"How do you manage? You don't seem like the mild and meek type."

"You've got that right. How do I manage? I remind him that my independence is one of the things he loves about me."

"Does that work?"

"Rarely. Distracting them works really well, though."

"What do you mean?"

"I'll show you."

Taking a new plate load of meat, Ellie sauntered on over to her husband. She placed her hand on his bare arm and leaned closer to whisper in his ear. Ben immediately stopped his argument with Rad and grinned down at his wife, tugging her closer to plant a kiss on her lips.

When Ellie returned to Serena she grinned. "See what I mean?"

"That won't work with Rad."

"Why not?"

Because the engagement wasn't real, so Rad wasn't vulnerable to her feminine wiles.

"Go ahead, try it." Ellie nudged her forward.

"No, I couldn't. Not in front of everyone." Serena would die of embarrassment if Rad rejected her, or worse looked at her with pity. She felt bad enough deceiving his lovely family.

"The pierogies are ready," Wanda announced from the kitchen behind them. "We are sitting down to eat now, yes?"

"Affirmative, *Busha*." Ben waved his metal prongs in the air before using them to rescue a steak from the grill. "Let's eat."

"Just remember what I told you," Rad cautioned him.

"I can't believe you did this. You, an intelligence officer, the 'answer man', and this was the best cover story you could come up with?"

"Shut up or someone will hear you."

"If you want this to work you need to stop looking so guilty."

Now Rad was really offended. Him? Look guilty? As if he were a wimp who wore his heart on his sleeve. There were those who even doubted he had a heart. He liked it that way. It made life less complicated.

"You know your problem?" Rad retorted. "You've been domesticated."

Rad could tell that Ben was now equally ticked-off. His older brother stepped forward, his chin thrust out.

Then he stopped as if some kind of internal light bulb had suddenly been switched on. Ben appeared dazed and then he just grinned stupidly. "Yeah, I guess I am domesticated. When I'm at home. And you know what? I like it. I downright love it. Having a wife who loves me and a child who makes every day brighter, oh yeah. I do downright love it."

"You're crazy."

"Crazy in love. Yeah. I am. You should try it."

Rad was horrified at the idea. "No way. I did that once." His voice was low yet sharp. "Never again."

"Liza would have wanted you to be happy."

"This isn't about her, it's about me."

"Are you two coming in or am I going to have to come out there?" Wanda demanded, her hands on her hips.

"We'll be there in a minute," Ben replied.

"We'll be in right now," Rad stated. "This conversation is over."

"Still the hothead in the family." Ben shook his head.

"Still trying to fix everyone's problems," Rad retorted.

Ben tossed an oven mitt at him.

"Oh, yeah," Rad scoffed. "Like that's gonna hurt me. I tell you, it's sad to see a fellow Marine like you lobbing oven mitts. What has the world come to?"

"Sorry, I left my hand grenades at the office," Ben drawled.

"I haven't, so don't mess with me."

Unable to hear their discussion, Serena watched the two men, so alike yet different. Both were extremely good-looking. But Ben had a more open nature than Rad.

They ate inside in the large great room off the kitchen. The meal was a study in organized chaos, with bowls laden with food being passed from hand to hand as multiple conversations went on at once. Her father would have a fit. She was surprised Rad wasn't ordering silence and demanding everyone speak in turn. He'd said it himself, he did not like chaos.

Yet there he sat, looking a little brooding at times, but not barking out any orders. He smiled at his niece often while she laughed or gazed at him adoringly as she was now.

Rad shook his head at Amy. "Stop batting your eyelashes at me, Princess. I am not going to talk your father into building a miniature golf course in your backyard."

"Why not?" Amy stuck out her bottom lip. Serena recognized the beginning of a pout. Her goddaughter Becky had been a pro at the maneuver.

"Because the miniature golf course is only a few miles down the highway."

"But I can't drive there."

"You've got that right."

"So I can't play whenever I want."

"And that's a tragedy to be sure," Wanda agreed sympathetically. "How about I teach you some new games after we eat?"

"What kinds of games?"

"The best kind."

"Which means it must be Polish," Rad noted dryly.

Wanda nodded. "*Granica* is similar to tug-of-war."

"Something Marines are very good at," Rad noted.

"Then we shall have one on each team."

Rad took his responsibilities as team leader very seriously. A glance over at Ben told her that he felt the same way. Both had intense expressions and were using that Marine voice. "Okay, listen up. *Busha* will give us instructions on how to play. Working together we can win this contest. Go ahead, *Busha*." Rad nodded at his grandmother.

"We hold on to a very long stick…" Wanda began.

"Daddy says Uncle Rad has to beat women off with a stick. Is that how we play this game?" Amy frowned her disapproval.

Wanda patted her shoulder reassuringly. "Your daddy was just using a figure of speech meaning that your uncle is popular with women. Beating women is a bad thing." She shot her grandsons a reprimanding look. "Right, Ben? Right, Rad?"

"Affirmative," both replied, their outraged expressions indicating their thoughts.

Ben added, "A strong man helps those in need."

"A strong man protects those in need," Rad stated.

Wanda smiled and nodded her approval before returning to a lengthy explanation of the game, which as far as Serena could tell, was just an adaptation of tug-of-war. Only in this case, a stick was used instead of a length of rope.

Rad and Ben were the first in line on their respective sides, then came Serena and Ellie and at the ends were Wanda and Amy.

"One to get ready," Amy shouted, having been assigned the role of starter. "Two to get set. And three to go!"

Minutes later the two Marines stared at their "troops" with dismay.

Rad spoke first. "You females laughed. You do not laugh in tug-of-war."

"It wasn't tug-of-war, it was *Granica*," Amy pointed out.

"It was a game," Ellie added.

Serena pointed out the positive. "Each side won once."

"Only because you laughed." Rad's voice was accusatory. "Otherwise our team would have won."

"No way," Ben scoffed. "*Our* team would have won."

"Did I mention that Marines are very competitive?" Ellie noted to Serena.

"Daddy…" Amy tugged on Ben's hand. "You told me that the important thing was to play the game well and give it your best effort."

"He was lying," Rad muttered.

Serena socked him. It seemed the right thing to do at the time. He responded by taking her hand in his and twining his fingers through hers.

"That's right." Ben bent down to give Amy a big hug.

"And to have fun. We had fun. That's why we were laughing," Amy explained.

"And because you guys looked so serious," Ellie added with a grin. "If you could have seen the look on your faces…"

"I always play to win," Rad said.

Serena tried to think of something clever to say, but she was distracted by the feel of his fingers holding hers. This was the first time they'd ever held hands. They'd already kissed but holding hands…was enough to make her go all rubbery-legged. Or maybe that was a result of playing tug-of-war.

No, she suspected it was Rad. Glancing down, she studied their hands. Her fingers looked so slender compared to his. He had wide palms with long, strong fingers. Even the way he held her hand indicated that this was a man who knew what he was doing, who was confident in his abilities.

She continued staring at their hands. Why didn't she feel trapped? She should feel trapped. But she didn't. Why was that? Was it the soothing rub of his thumb? Was it the loose way he held her? She felt joined with him. What did he feel?

She glanced up, wondering if he'd even noticed that his fingers were still entwined with hers. But his gaze was on Amy as he teased her about something.

Suddenly, the enormity of her lie caught up with her. When the rest of the family headed inside for ice cream, Serena held Rad back.

"What's the matter?"

She freed her fingers. She needed to think clearly. She needed to remember that this wasn't real. "Can't you tell them the truth?"

Rad shook his head. "It's too late now. They already think you're my fiancée. Trust me, my grandmother would not understand. And she's not capable of keeping a secret. You're doing great so far." He cupped her face, brushing his thumb against her cheek. "Just hang in there."

"Do you want chocolate or strawberry ice cream?" Amy called out.

"Both," Rad called back with a grin. "And hot fudge and whipped cream on top."

An hour later, Serena was in Rad's car on her way

back to her real life. The silence made her feel awkward. "They seem like a really nice couple."

"They didn't always have it easy. Ellie's brother was under Ben's command when he was killed by friendly fire. For a long time, Ben held himself responsible even though he didn't fire the shot. But he believed that her brother had taken a bullet meant for him."

"That must have been difficult."

"Yeah, but they got over it. What doesn't kill you makes you tougher."

"And you're all for being tough, aren't you?"

"I'm a Marine. It goes with the territory."

She knew that. Being tough and being bossy were all part of the deal, part of the package.

"You have a nice family." Unlike her own. "I feel badly deceiving them this way."

"It's for a good cause."

His calm words irritated her. "Your career in the military?"

"I was referring to your bookstore."

What could she say to that? It was true that she'd agreed to this plan because of her bookstore. But that was before. Before she'd met his grandmother. Before she'd kissed Rad. Before she'd experienced his seductive ways.

"We have nothing in common," Serena said abruptly.

Rad pulled the Corvette into the parking space behind her building before replying. "You wouldn't know that from the way we kissed earlier."

"That can't happen again."

"We're pretending to be an engaged couple. Kissing comes with the territory."

"Not that kind of kissing." Not the kind that melted her soul.

Turning, he leaned toward her. His gaze was a clear challenge. So was his slow smile. "Then show me what kind of kissing you prefer."

Serena could tell that he thought she'd hop out of the car in outrage. Instead she decided to call his bluff. "This kind." She meant to bestow a polite kiss on his cheek, but he turned his head at the last moment and her lips met his.

Chapter Six

Serena was amazed at how quickly something so innocent could turn so seductive. All it took was the touch of his lips on hers, the thrust of his fingers through her hair as he angled her head to ensure ultimate satisfaction.

His mouth engulfed hers in a turbulent and erotic game of tongue tag, making her forget all the valid reasons she shouldn't be doing this. She couldn't think; she could only feel.

Excitement surged through her as a whirlpool of sensations sucked her into this forbidden world of dark seduction. The intensity of the pleasure he aroused within her—the edgy need, the wanton desire—consumed her entirely.

One kiss blended into the next, each one escalating in intimacy, pulling her deeper and deeper into his embrace. Catching her bottom lip between his teeth, Rad drew it into his mouth to suck and nibble until her sighs became moans.

His talented hands were equally skillful. He braced her head with one hand while allowing his right hand to slide down her throat, past her collarbone. He brushed his thumb against her skin, his touch tantalizingly tender compared to the hunger of his kiss. She rested her hands on his broad shoulders, awed by the sheer bulk of him in these tight confines.

Serena wasn't sure how his hand stole beneath her top but it did. Seconds later he was reverently cupping her breast in his palm, teasing her nipple with the tip of his thumb. She shivered at the delicious caress that both inflamed and incited. She was totally swept away by the tidal wave of sensual desire.

She needed to get closer to him. She squirmed, her derriere sliding against the black leather bucket seat as she tried to erase the space between them. Instead she ended up banging her knee on the gearshift console.

Gasping she pulled away, tears coming to her eyes.

"Are you okay?" Rad asked her.

Serena shook her head. Of course she wasn't okay. She'd just made out with him in the front seat of his Corvette.

"Let me help—"

"Stay away from me!" Dismayed by her lack of control, Serena jumped out of the car. Her knee throbbed as she ran up to her apartment but that was nothing compared to the throbbing in her heart as she realized how quickly her business arrangement with Rad had turned dangerously personal.

* * *

Serena had everything ready for the book signing. She felt confident that today would be a huge success. Customers were lined up outside the door, just waiting to come in and buy books. Lots of books.

Time to let them in. She punched the code into the security system but nothing happened. Her heart started pounding and so did the impatient people outside, bamming their fists on the glass windows and door.

Serena's fingers trembled as she frantically entered the numbers on the keypad again. Nothing. What could be wrong?

"Discipline!" Rad, in full dress blues, barked from her side. "Discipline is a critical part of being a Marine and of succeeding in life. Without discipline there's chaos. Marines do *not* like chaos."

"I'm the radical one in the family," Rad, in jeans and a white T-shirt, whispered in her ear on her other side. He swirled his index finger around the curve of her ear and down her neck. He undid the lower half of the buttons on her dress while the uniformed Rad efficiently dispatched the top buttons.

Outside the store, the crowd watched with ogle-eyed anticipation as the two Rads, the officer and the bad boy, caressed her body.

"I'm Serena Serious," she told them both.

"We want Serena Sensuous to come out and play."

"I can't. Not with all these people…"

A second later the crowd was gone and so were her clothes as Serena found herself in bed with just one Rad. A very naked Rad. "Which one are you?" she whispered while running her hands over his bare chest.

"The one you want."

This was more than mere *want,* this was *had to have right now!*

Rad fueled that flame by erotically touching her, there…where she ached, where her body was moist and welcoming. His sliding fingers created a glorious friction that had her gripping the bedclothes. Seconds later she transferred her hold to his wide shoulders as he lowered his mouth to her bare breast. Slivers of sheer bliss pinwheeled out of control as he swirled his tongue over her nipple while brushing his thumb over her feminine treasure trove. She exploded, her entire being pulsating in a never-ending series of contractions.

She gasped for breath…and woke up.

She was alone in her bed. It had all been a dream. An incredibly powerful dream.

She closed her eyes. Maybe it would come back….

A second later, the buzzing of the alarm dragged her back to reality before she even had a chance to bask in the afterglow.

This was what she got for kissing a sexy Marine and then staying awake half the night brooding about it while reading the Sexual Goddess's latest book before falling asleep. Specifically, the chapter on *Finding Sexual Satisfaction.*

So she'd dreamt that Rad had made love to her. So what? It didn't mean anything.

This was just another lie heaped on top of all the rest.

"Where do you want the rest of these chairs?" Clay asked her two hours later. They'd already transformed one corner of the store over by the benched alcove into a seating area for forty people. Folded chairs stood at attention, ready to do their duty.

Great, now even the chairs were getting military overtones. Serena tried not to let her thoughts wander that way. "I think we can fit one more row back here if we move this display rack."

Clay took care of that. "You're expecting a lot of people to come to this thing today?"

"I hope so."

He nervously tugged on his Blink-182 T-shirt. "What about that girl who was in here the other day?"

"Which one?"

"The awesome one. Dark hair, bodacious eyes."

"I have no idea if Heidi will be here."

"It's possible though, right?"

"Anything is possible where Heidi is concerned."

"Who's Heidi?" Kalinda demanded as she set a glass punch bowl filled with lemonade on a table nearby.

"No one," Clay muttered before setting up the remaining chairs.

Serena had borrowed them from the church a few blocks away. In return, she did book sales for their special events.

A tap at the still locked door got Serena's attention. All she saw was a gorgeous array of flowers. It had to be Jane from the florist shop next door.

Serena opened the door, trying to ignore the memory of her dream of herself standing before this very door with Rad undoing her dress. She licked lips that had suddenly gone bone dry. "Uh, you and Hosea have really outdone yourself this time." Hosea, Jane's husband, was also her partner in the business. He was also incredibly talented, creating some of the most memorable floral designs that Serena had ever seen.

This one certainly ranked right up there. Filled with splashes of her favorite colors—reds and yellows and oranges.

"Yes, we did. But this isn't for your book signing." The store did the arrangements at a discount, and in return Serena handed out discount coupons for a bouquet of flowers. It was a way for the two businesses to complement one another and both increase business.

"So you just brought these over to show them off? I can understand why. They are outstanding."

"They're for you."

"But you just said—"

"That they weren't for the signing. That's right. Hosea is still working on that arrangement. It's much smaller than this one. These are for you personally."

"You guys shouldn't have…"

"We didn't. The flowers were sent to you by an admirer."

While Serena and Jane had been talking, Kalinda had cleared a space for the terra cotta container. "Set them here. There's a card," she added for Serena's benefit. "Aren't you going to open it?"

Serena eyed the small white rectangle as if it were Pandora's box and opening it would result in all her inner sexual fantasies pouring out. "Later. I'll…uh…open it later."

"Don't you want to know who they're from?" Kalinda prompted.

"Probably from the publisher," the pragmatic Clay stated. "Thanking you for all the work you're doing for this signing."

Serena laughed at herself for being such a fool. Clay was probably right. The flowers were from the Sexual Goddess's publisher. Not from the inciter of Serena Sensuous.

Serena opened the card. She instantly recognized the bold slash of the letters. She'd seen them before. In Rad's signature on the contract he'd offered her.

Good luck today. Thinking of you, Rad.

"What does it say?" Kalinda asked. "Who are they from?"

Serena was saved from answering that question by the arrival of their first group of customers as Kalinda unlocked the door. Because of the more adult content of today's program, Serena had opened the store for attendees only, opening to her regular customers afterward. She was surprised to find that Rad's grandmother was the first person in line. The older woman hadn't said anything about actually attending today's event.

"Are we too early?" Wanda asked. "I didn't want to get here too late to get a seat."

"You're fine. As you can see, we still have plenty of room." She didn't know what else to say.

"My, those are lovely flowers."

"Yes." Serena stuffed the card in the pocket of her dress.

Seeming to take pity on her flustered boss, Kalinda distracted the newcomers by offering them paper cups of lemonade and cookies. Serena hurried away to finish other preparations. By the time she'd returned several minutes later, a majority of the seats were taken.

Despite all the publicity and the ads in the paper she'd placed, Serena never knew if a signing would be successful or not. She was relieved that this appeared to be a hit.

"Serena?"

She turned to find Ellie Kozlowski standing by the lemonade. "I hope you don't mind us coming. I brought along some of my friends." She pointed to two women in the third row seated beside Wanda. They waved.

That's not all they did. After Amelia Smith aka the Sexual Goddess completed her presentation and asked for questions from the audience, Wanda was the first to comply. "My grandson Rad has just gotten engaged to Serena here." Wanda patted Serena's arm. "Do you have any words of advice for the young couple?"

Serena could only stand by, a silent observer of her own train wreck as all her loyal customers cheered and clapped their congratulations.

The news of her fictional engagement was like the small snowball that rolled into a huge avalanche, gaining momentum and speed until it consumed everything in its path.

When she'd first agreed to this plan, only a few days ago yet a lifetime away, she'd warned Rad that things could get complicated. But not even she had anticipated the news spreading so that her professional life would be affected.

The first hug came from Kalinda. "Why haven't I met this guy yet?"

"I was trying to keep my private life private."

"Not with this crowd."

"Words of advice?" Amelia the author said. "Communicate. Talk to each other. The more comforting, positive, humorous, loving words you use, the better. But there are times when you just want to live in the moment, and savor it, without over-thinking things. You've heard the phrase never go to bed mad? It's right. And if your schedule allows, you may want to make love in the morning, when the male testosterone level is at its highest."

"Okay, then." Serena smiled brightly, even though she could feel her cheeks burning. She couldn't believe she'd just been told when to make love while Rad's grandmother listened in. "Let's break for some refreshments and so that you can get your own autographed copy of Amelia Smith's book."

Serena tried but she didn't get away quickly enough. Her exit was blocked by two women, the two that Ellie had indicated earlier were friends of hers. "Hi, I'm Latesha."

"And I'm Cyn. We're Ellie's friends. Latesha is a newlywed so she can give advice. I'm still looking for that perfect man."

"In all the wrong places," Latesha shot back. "What were you thinking dating that guy from the strip club?"

Cyn just grinned. "I was thinking that he looked mighty fine in a jock strap."

"Just be glad you don't have these two planning your bachelorette party," Ellie told Serena as she placed an arm around both friends' shoulders. "They held mine at a male strip club and invited my future mother-in-law. She was a good sport about it, but I thought I'd die."

Latesha rolled her eyes. "Ellie is such a drama queen."

"And since she's happily married to that fine-looking Marine of hers, she's gotten even more impossible,"

Cyn noted with a fond grin. "And now you're engaged to a fine-looking Marine of your own, Serena. Lucky you! We saw Rad at Ellie's wedding. He caught the garter just a few months ago when Ellie and Ben renewed their vows for their first wedding anniversary."

"She heard the story last night when she came to our house for dinner. But we shouldn't monopolize your time this way," Ellie noted apologetically. "There are lots of people waiting to congratulate you."

Next in line were Heather and Tiana, two of Serena's most loyal customers. They were part of the romance reader group that Serena had started a few months ago and two of the nicest people she'd ever met. Tiana was a paralegal and Heather a teacher happily married to a handsome lawyer.

"So when's the wedding?" Heather asked. "Have you set a date yet?"

Serena just shook her head. Their honest excitement and joy over her "good news" ripped open Serena's scab of guilt. What kind of person was she to lie like this? She'd sold her soul to the devil for fifty percent off on her rent.

She stood there, frozen, as people continued to hug her and congratulate her.

Inside she was overwhelmed by it all, falling deeper and deeper into a well of panic.

Rad wasn't doing so well himself. Heidi had once again confronted him at work. At least she hadn't ambushed him this time. He'd seen her coming but had had no time to escape.

"I've been looking all over for you." She said the

words as if accusing him of deliberately hiding from her. "I got the greatest idea."

He was afraid to ask, and he wasn't a man who was afraid of much. He was sure whatever her idea, he wouldn't like it.

"I'm going to throw a huge engagement party for you and Sabrina."

Yep, he didn't like the idea one bit. "Her name is Serena and we don't need a party, thank you, ma'am." He deliberately kept his tone extremely formal.

"You don't want a party?"

"Affirmative, ma'am."

"And why is that?"

"Excuse me?"

"Why don't you want a party? Most couples would be happy to have a party in their honor."

"Serena and I aren't most couples."

"I noticed that."

The general's daughter was wearing that suspicious look again.

"It's just that I like keeping my private life quiet."

"That's what Serena said."

"You talked to her about having a party?" She'd skin him alive. Not that Rad was worried about her anger. He was a Marine, he could handle anything thrown his way. But juggling his stories between these females was getting complicated and requiring more effort than he'd anticipated.

"No, I didn't talk to her about this. I wanted to talk to you first."

"Good."

She beamed. "So you're glad I came to talk to you?"

"I'm glad you talked to me first about the party so I could head you off at the pass."

"What does that mean?"

"It means I don't want a party, thank you anyway, ma'am."

"What if Serena wants one?"

"She doesn't."

"How do you know? Have you asked her?"

"I don't have to ask her. I know how she thinks." Not true or he'd know why she'd taken off as if chased by a SCUD missile after they'd made out in his Corvette. Not that the bucket seats made for the easiest location for such activities. But he hadn't cared. He'd been so into their kiss that he'd lost track of everything else.

"Maybe I should talk to her," Heidi was saying.

"No, I don't think that's a good idea."

"Why not? Are you afraid she'll say something she shouldn't?"

"Negative." He fell back on his military terminology. "As I said, we thank you for the offer, but my fiancée and I prefer to spend our time together as a couple at this time."

Heidi just shrugged.

When Rad's phone rang, he reached forward to answer it, glad for the interruption. By the time he'd completed the call, Heidi had left. Another land mine successfully avoided.

"Don't even think about it," Serena warned Bella as the cat strolled over to her water dish with her toy in her mouth. "Do not drop that in there...."

Plop. Too late. Bella glanced at Serena with a satisfied grin. Gotcha!

So much for Serena being in charge. She couldn't even get her cats to behave. What chance did she have with a sexy Marine?

Serena fished the soaked fuzzy toy out and squeezed the excess moisture from it.

Bella gave that special small meow that, translated, meant, That's mine, throw it to me. *Now!*

Serena tossed it and had to laugh as Bella's paws skidded on the wood floor as she tried to gain traction, making her look like one of those cartoon characters with the pinwheeling feet.

Bella brought the toy back and dropped it at Serena's feet. While they played this retrieving game, Serena told the more serene Oshi about the disaster of her day. "The book signing went well. We sold all the books we had. But now everybody thinks I'm engaged. I should have anticipated something like this happening. It feels like my life isn't my own anymore."

Oshi purred her understanding and rubbed her head against Serena's leg.

Serena was letting her answering machine screen her calls, but when she heard Lucy's voice, she picked up.

"So how is the pseudo-engagement going?" her friend inquired.

"Terrible." Serena curled onto the couch, making herself comfortable. She had a feeling this conversation would take a while because she needed to talk. "I met his family last night."

"I didn't know that was part of the deal."

"It wasn't."

"Typical. You give the guy an inch and he takes a mile. How bad was his family?"

"They weren't bad at all. They were great. I felt like such an evil person for lying to them. His grandmother thinks I'm three-quarters Polish."

"Are you?"

"I have no idea."

"Then why does she think that?"

"Because Rad told her."

"Then he's the one who should be feeling guilty, not you."

Serena paused before admitting, "He kissed me."

"The rat buzzard."

"I liked it. *A lot*."

"Uh-oh."

"I totally melted. Like butter. He's an incredible kisser."

"Great technique, huh?"

"Five star."

"Wow."

"Yeah."

"So what are you going to do now?"

"Take a bath and go to bed. I had the book signing today and I'm beat. I didn't sleep well last night."

"He stayed the night?"

"No, he didn't. But I kept thinking about him all night."

"Not a good sign."

"Tell me about it."

"No, you tell me about it. Maybe you were just caught unprepared by his first kiss. Maybe his next one will be—"

"It was even better." Serena got up and headed for the kitchen, reaching into the freezer for some ice cream. She only had Cherry Garcia, but she'd make do.

"He kissed you twice?"

"Yeah." Serena skipped the bowl and dug right into the pint container with a spoon.

"Like twice in a row, or two totally separate occasions?"

"Two totally separate occasions."

"Did he sneak up on you?"

"The second time I kissed him."

"What for?"

"I was trying to prove a point."

"Which was?"

"Never mind. It didn't work anyway."

"That sort of thing rarely does. So how did he respond?"

"Oh, he responded just fine. I'm the one who went racing from his car like a thirteen-year-old on her first date."

"You were making out in his car?"

"He has a Corvette."

"Oh that explains it then," Lucy noted mockingly. "You always make out with guys who drive Corvettes. Especially if they're bossy Marines."

"I know, I know." She brought the ice cream with her and plopped back onto the couch again. "This is all so totally unlike me."

"Is he using the discount in your rent to try and make it with you?"

"No, that's not it at all. He's not applying any undue pressure or trying to twist my arm to get me to do anything I don't want to do. That's the problem. I *wanted* to kiss him. I *wanted* his arms around me. Then I panicked."

"Why?"

"Because, as you said, he's a bossy Marine." Deciding she needed to display some willpower here, Serena set the ice cream aside. "I don't intend to follow in my mother's footsteps and become subservient to an autocrat. I mean, come on. Rad and I have nothing in common."

"Aside from liking to kiss one another, you mean?"

Serena sighed. "What am I going to do?"

"You're asking me?"

"Of course I am. You're my best friend. Giving advice is your job."

"If you don't want to get involved with him, then don't kiss him anymore."

Serena bit her bottom lip. "Am I a bad person?"

"Of course not! Where did that come from?"

"His family is so nice." Serena knew her voice sounded wistful but there was nothing she could do about it. "His brother is married to a woman who has a six-year-old daughter. And his grandmother is a real sweetie. She gave me her secret recipe for pierogies. She's very proud of being Polish. She'll hate me when she finds out I lied to her."

"How is she going to find out?"

"I don't know. I just have this sick feeling in the pit of my stomach that this charade is going to come undone and that it will all be my fault."

Rad jiggled the bag of Chinese take-out he held and dialed Serena's number again. It had been busy for half an hour. He couldn't believe she didn't have call-waiting or caller ID or something. Unless she knew it was him and was trying to avoid him?

Too bad. They had things to discuss. And there was no time like the present.

The line rang and this time he got her answering machine. He glanced up at the light in her windows. "I know you're there. Pick up, Serena."

She did. "Hello?"

"I'm outside your building with food. Well, actually I'm now halfway up the stairs."

"What kind of food?"

"Chinese. From your favorite place. Your assistant told me what you like. Egg rolls plus walnut shrimp and scallops."

Serena unlocked the door and let him in. She was interested in the food, not in him, she told herself. Yeah, right.

He looked good. Rad always looked good. It didn't matter if he was wearing his Marine uniform or jeans and a T-shirt. He was just that kind of a guy. The kind that could steal a woman's heart without even trying.

Denim had been invented for men like him, ones with muscular legs and awesome butts.

She watched him walk past her and tried not to drool. She told herself she was salivating over the smell of her favorite Chinese food, but it was Rad that she wanted to nibble on.

She remembered how he'd sucked her bottom lip into his mouth and taken delicious little nibbles while kissing her.

Lack of sleep must be weakening her defenses. She'd only gotten a few hours rest last night, and that had been haunted by the hot dreams she'd had. In fact, this entire week had disrupted her usual sleep pattern.

Hey, that sounded like something Serena Serious would say.

Which meant that Serena Sensual was back under control again.

She hoped…

Rad paused as two streaks of gray flew past him.

"My two cats," Serena explained. "Oshi and Bella. They're shy."

So was Serena. At times. Rad only now realized that, despite her hot response to his kisses. Serena was not a man-eater. Not like Heidi.

Serena was different. Complicated. She had a way about her. She did things to him. Her smile, the way she walked, the softness of her hair, her laugh. They all did things to him. Serious, call-in-reinforcements kinds of things. Mushy, sappy, un-Marine-like things.

"I'll get some plates," Serena said.

Rad watched her walk away. She was wearing some kind of soft-knit cotton pants and a matching tank top that looked like they could be slept in. Nothing fancy. Totally casual.

His heightened sense of observation took note of the fact that her bare skin showed between the top and bottom of her outfit.

That brief glimpse of the small of her back had the power to make him all hot and bothered.

This was a new experience for him. Women had been eager to display their bodies to him before.

But not this woman. This woman had the power to mess up his mind with the slightest of things.

Like the way she ate. She had a healthy appetite, he had to give her that. He watched as she finished off her egg rolls and dug into the walnut shrimp and scallops. His mouth was too dry to talk much, hers was too full.

Afterward, Rad cleared the table and ordered her to rest on the couch. He knew she was exhausted because she actually obeyed him for once. It was time he told her his big news.

He returned from the living room to find Serena laid out on her couch, sound asleep.

There was only one thing he could do….

Chapter Seven

Serena sat up, her heart pounding in her throat, unsure what woke her.

Then she heard the noise again.

Footsteps.

Directly above her bed.

Wait a second! Disoriented, she looked around. The last thing she remembered, she'd laid down on the couch in the living room. How had she gotten into bed?

Rad. He must have carried her into her bedroom.

Okay, that was one mystery solved.

She was still wearing the same clothes, thank heavens, which meant he hadn't stripped her and put her in a negligee. That was a good thing.

But none of that explained the noise from upstairs. The third-floor apartment had been vacant since Mrs. Schuler had moved out a month ago.

Serena quickly glanced at the LED display on the radio/alarm beside her bed. Two in the morning.

Oshi and Bella lifted their heads and stared up at the ceiling. As the footsteps moved again, both cats bolted under the bed. Serena grabbed for the phone and dialed 911.

"Someone has broken into the apartment above me," she whispered to the dispatcher even as she hopped out of bed and quietly hurried to make sure all the dead bolts on her apartment door were latched. They were.

She also checked the door from the kitchen that led out onto the fire escape. Bolted, too. Good.

She gave her information to the police and was assured that officers would be there shortly. As she talked, Serena walked back and forth, too nervous to sit still.

All the while she kept the lights off. She didn't want the intruder upstairs noticing any sudden illumination coming from her place. A night-light in the hallway allowed her to see where she was going.

Exactly eight minutes later there was an emphatic knock on her door. "Police. Officer Krandell." That was the name that the dispatcher had given her.

Even so, Serena looked through the peephole in her front door before undoing the locks and opening it. She also turned on a light. "Did you catch the intruder?"

"He says he owns the building."

Serena blinked. "What?"

"I can't believe you called the police," Rad growled. He was glaring at her, his expression one of classic male aggravation.

How dare he try and make this her fault. "What else

was I supposed to do when I hear noises coming from a vacant apartment?"

"It's not vacant any more. I'm moving into it."

"In the middle of the night?"

"Ma'am, can you verify that this man, Rad Kozlowski, is indeed the building owner?"

Serena nodded. "Yes."

"I'm also her fiancé," Rad added, not appreciating the way the young cop was eyeing Serena.

"Is that right, ma'am?" the officer asked.

"Unfortunately, yes."

"Did you two have an argument?"

"No."

Officer Krandell nodded at his partner who took Rad aside.

"Do you mind if I come inside for a moment, ma'am?"

"No, I don't mind. Can I make you some coffee or something?"

"No, thank you." Officer Krandell closed the door behind him, shutting Rad and his protests outside in the hallway. "I just wanted to make sure you're okay?"

"I'm still a little nervous."

"Why is that?"

"Because hearing those footsteps over my bed in the middle of the night scared me. I'm sorry I called you out here for nothing."

"You're sure you're not afraid of the Marine out there? Your fiancé?"

"He told you he's a Marine?"

"Captain Rad Kozlowski. Yes, ma'am. But you still haven't answered my question."

She was disconcerted by the way Rad made her feel, but she wasn't afraid of him.

"Ma'am?"

"I'm sorry. It's just that it's been a long day. I had a big book signing at my store downstairs today, and then they found out about my engagement and started giving me advice… Never mind, that's way more information than you wanted, I'm sure. No, Officer Krandell. I'm definitely not afraid of Rad. Aggravated with him for scaring me this way, but not afraid of him."

"You're sure? Because there are family outreach services that can help you.…"

"I'm fine. Really. If I'd known it was Rad upstairs I never would have called the police. Again, I'm sorry to have bothered you."

"No bother, ma'am. That's our job." The officer opened the door. "Okay, it looks like we're done here. Next time, you might want to let your fiancée know your plans ahead of time," Officer Krandell told Rad before leaving.

"What are you doing here sneaking around in the middle of the night?" Serena demanded.

"Let me in and I'll tell you."

When she hesitated, Rad became even more aggravated. "What? You trust a total stranger and let him come into your apartment but you don't trust me?"

"What total stranger?"

"That cop that was eyeing you."

"He was not eyeing me, he was just doing his job."

"Oh, he was eyeing you, alright. Trust me, I know."

"I'm sure you do."

"What's that supposed to mean?"

"That I'm sure you've eyed plenty of women."

"So?"

"So, you have your nerve accusing that poor police officer of something you do yourself at every opportunity."

"Are you accusing me of eyeing you at every opportunity?"

"I meant you eye other women."

"What other women?"

"Never mind. You still haven't told me what you're doing here in the middle of the night."

"I'm moving in."

"Where?"

"Where do you think? Into the apartment upstairs."

"Why?"

"Because it's empty."

"So get a renter. Put an ad in the paper."

"Why, Serena darlin'," he drawled. "If I didn't know better I'd think you didn't want me to move in."

"You're right. I don't want you moving in."

Her words stung. "I own the building. I don't need your permission to do anything."

"You may own the building, but you don't own me!"

She slammed the door in his face. Or tried to. His outstretched hand stopped the door from closing.

"What are you so mad about?"

"You! I'm mad about you." Wait a second, that hadn't come out right. "I mean I'm angry with you." Then, because she was tired and fired up, she added, "You're just like my father."

"Hold on a second. Where did that come from?"

"Go away!"

"No, I'm not going away until you explain this to me."

Serena was so upset she had to walk away. Unfortunately, that left the door open for him to walk through.

"Did your dad hit you? Is that why you've got this thing—"

She angrily turned on him. "I don't have a thing. And I already told you he didn't hit me any more than any dad would. He didn't have to. His words were as powerful as a punch. He was a control freak. Everything had to be done his way or else. I've already told you that I don't like being bossed around, but you do it anyway. I ask you to leave, but you ignore me. You don't listen. Just like him. He never listened either."

"Wait a minute…" Rad protested.

"No, I'm not waiting. And I'm not letting anyone else ever control me again. I'd like you to leave now."

To her surprise, Rad did as she asked. But he warned her, "This isn't over."

By eleven o'clock the next morning, Rad realized he may not have handled things very well. He saw no resemblance between himself and the man Serena had described her father to be. He should have picked up on her issues, but they'd been so wrapped up in his family lately that he hadn't thought about Serena's.

Her dad had clearly left scars.

Being ordered around was a red-hot button for Serena. He supposed he could understand that.

Everyone had their triggers, something that set them off. That didn't mean it was logical, however.

One thing he did know, he'd gotten jealous when that

young cop had eyed Serena last night. He'd wanted to stake a claim on her, to tell everyone she was his.

Okay, so maybe that made him a caveman throw-back.

In his view, it just made him a guy.

But it was Serena's view that mattered here, too.

So maybe he needed to adapt his battle plan. Maybe he needed to sway her over to his way of thinking, that they were good together.

And he definitely needed that ring on her finger, pronto.

And so it was that Rad came knocking on her door at eleven o'clock on Sunday morning, with a sack of freshly made doughnuts in hand. A peace offering from the bakery down the block.

He had a hard time reading her expression when she opened the door, but she did seem interested in the doughnuts. And she let him in—surely that was a good thing?

Rad started off by apologizing. Women loved that. "I'm sorry I scared you last night. I meant to tell you after dinner that I was moving in, but you fell asleep."

"You put me to bed?"

"That's right. I didn't think you wanted to spend the night on the couch."

"It wouldn't be the first time." During those weeks when she'd first opened the store, Serena had fallen asleep studying spreadsheets of expenses and income.

"Do you accept my apology?"

She nodded and finished the last bite of her dough-nut. She was only having one.

"Good. Then we'll head out now."

"Wait a minute. Head out where?"

"To get the engagement ring."

"I can do that myself."

"You could, but you didn't. So we're going together."

Anger flashed in her green eyes. "There you go, ordering me around again."

"Stop trying to get out of our agreement."

"I am not doing that."

"And I am not being bossy. I simply do whatever is necessary for my mission to have a successful outcome."

"So the end justifies the means? No matter who gets hurt in the process? Just collateral damage, right?"

Rad frowned. "How did we go from buying a ring to collateral damage?"

"Because you have no regrets about ordering people around. But then, that's what you do for a living, isn't it. Give orders. But guess what? That doesn't work with me. I'm an independent woman with a mind of her own."

"Who wants what? A fancy invitation to go get this stupid ring? Can we just get this over with?"

"I've already told you that you don't have to come with me at all."

"And I've told you, I'm coming. So let's go."

She rolled her eyes at him.

Rad reminded himself of his new plan, the one that he'd forgotten in the heat of the male-female battle. "Let's go...*please*. Does that make you happy?"

"Having this entire thing over with would make me happy."

"Pizza and a cold beer would make me happy, as I

think I've told you before. But hey, we can't always have what we want. So are you ready to go?"

"You should have called first."

"I brought doughnuts."

"That isn't a get-out-of-jail-free card, you know."

Too bad. Rad cooled his heels while Serena took her time getting ready. Or maybe it just seemed that way to him. She really only took fifteen minutes.

During that time she'd pinned her hair away from her face, leaving most of it loose. He liked the way her jeans fit and her READ T-shirt drew his attention to her breasts. He noticed her toenails were painted a racy red and that the heels on her sandals brought her an inch higher than usual.

Which put her lips in even closer proximity to his mouth as she turned to face him. "I'm ready now."

He'd been ready since the first moment he'd spotted her in that crowded gymnasium at the school, standing at the back, wearing that red dress and eyeing him with disapproval. Ready to kiss her, ready to put his arms around her and carry her off to his bed.

Rad watched Serena get into his car while he held the door open for her. His thoughts remained on her sexy denim-clad legs as he pulled the Corvette into traffic.

"Heidi is suspicious."

Serena's comment dissolved his fantasy in an instant. "What did she say?"

"It wasn't what she said, it was the way she acted."

"Obsessive, you mean?"

"Suspicious."

"What did you do?"

She raised an eyebrow at him. "Is that your way of implying that I somehow messed up?"

"It's my way of trying to ascertain the facts."

"I didn't do anything."

"Has she been back to the store?"

"No."

"She didn't come to that sex goddess thing yesterday?"

"No. Your grandmother did, though."

"You didn't tell me that."

"Turn right here."

"Why?"

"Because that's where the discount store is. They sell rings."

Twenty minutes later, Rad finally found a parking space in the crowded parking lot, one that was far enough away that his Corvette wouldn't get dinged by some stupid shopping cart.

He reluctantly followed Serena into the mega-store. Shopping. That ranked right up there with dentist visits and athlete's foot in his book.

The jewelry counter was located in the middle of the store. Serena was telling the sales clerk that she wanted something inexpensive, when Rad looked up to spot someone he recognized.

A fellow Marine. Someone in his command.

"We've got to go." He hustled Serena out of the store.

"Why? What's wrong?"

"I'm not buying a ring in there. And have it spread all over the base that I bought you a cheap ring? No way."

"So now what?"

He almost said *We do this my way*, but then realized she might take offense to that.

Instead he drove to a jewelry store they'd passed on the way.

"Do you want to come in?"

She shook her head. "This was your idea."

He was back in the time it took Serena to play two songs on the CD he had in the CD player—one was called *No Shirt, No Shoes, No Problem.*

"Here." He handed her the box.

She opened it to find a classy emerald-cut diamond ring with two smaller channel-set diamonds on either side.

"Do you like it?"

She had to nod. Who wouldn't love a ring like this?

"It's real, no Cubic Zirconias, and it's fully insured so you don't have to worry about losing it or anything. Does it fit?" He lifted it from the case and reached for her hand.

The slide of the ring over her finger, the feel of his hand holding hers, the way he bent his head to watch what he was doing—these were all images from a real engagement, from a man presenting the woman he loved with a token of his intentions to spend the rest of his life with her.

She swallowed the sudden lump in her throat.

The ring fit.

Perfectly.

Her eyes met his. The intensity she saw there caught her by surprise.

Then he smiled, that slow smile that made the lines at the corners of his brown eyes crinkle. "Mission accomplished."

If his mission had been to invade her heart, it looked like he was succeeding.

She had to display some common sense here, some caution.

But all she seemed to be able to do was nod.

"Good." He turned and started the car.

Within moments she realized they weren't headed back to her apartment. "Where are we going now?"

"To get paint. Did you know that the previous renter painted the bedroom walls the most disgusting pink color? Marines don't have pink bedrooms."

Serena wondered how many engaged women went from the jewelry store to the hardware store. But then this wasn't a normal engagement.

This time she didn't stay in the car. She went into the huge home-improvement warehouse with him.

The overhead lights made her ring sparkle and dance with light. She had a hard time keeping her eyes off it and kept glancing down at her left hand.

Okay, time to get real here, to stop daydreaming. "What color were you thinking of getting?" She pointed to the impressive display of chromatic choices.

Rad didn't even bother looking at any of them. Instead he made a beeline straight for a shelf and grabbed a couple of gallons to put in the shopping cart Serena had snared on their way in.

She looked at the label and then at him. "Wimp."

That finally got his attention. "What?"

"You're a color wimp. Beige. Bland, bland, bland."

"It's better than pink."

"A real man would choose a dark blue or green. But that's probably too much color for you to handle."

Rad put his hands on his hips, a classic Marine

stance. "I can handle color as long as it's a macho color and not some girly pink or purple."

"No pinks or purples," she promised him, taking his arm and tugging him over to the display area where row upon row of color swatches created a virtual rainbow of choices.

Rad warned, "I don't have all day to stand around...."

"Here." She pointed to a rich blue color and then briskly moved the cart down to the area where the paint was custom blended.

"Contentment?" He read over her shoulder. "What kind of name is that for a paint color?"

"A positive one." After placing her order, Serena watched the machine that shook the paint up with the realization that that's how Rad made her feel. All shook up.

From the first moment she'd seen him, he'd gotten to her. Even when she'd stood in the back of the school gymnasium, he'd gotten to her.

She'd chalked it up to aggravation from his gung-ho approach and lack of sensitivity, but now she wondered if she'd just been fooling herself.

There was no denying that Rad was a man who got women's attention. Even now, the young female sales clerk who worked the paint area was eyeing him with appreciation, smiling and asking if he needed any help.

Serena was the one who needed help. The more time she spent with him, the more she was attracted to him.

She glanced down at the ring on her hand. It felt strange, yet oddly comforting.

She touched it with her right index finger, as if to

confirm that a beautiful engagement ring really did rest on her left finger.

Serena couldn't allow herself to get all sappy here. The ring might be real, but the engagement wasn't.

A few minutes later, the paint was ready. "Take that wimpy beige out and put these gallons in instead."

"I'll get both," Rad said.

"So much for being the radical one in the family," Serena scoffed. "You need your beige security blanket."

He couldn't remove the paint gallons from the cart fast enough.

Serena tried not to smile. He was such a *guy*. Being accused of any sign of weakness got them every time.

Not that she thought Rad was vulnerable in any way. He was one of the most confident men she'd ever met. It was there even now in the way he held himself, in his regally erect posture, in the strength he projected.

Two hours later, Serena stood back from the wall they'd painted and nodded approvingly. "That looks really good."

"Really good." But Rad was looking at her, not the wall, when he said that.

"Oh, yeah, I'm a regular fashion plate in my paint-splattered clothes." She'd secured her ring on a long chain around her neck—tucked between her breasts, secure against her heart, and safe from paint splatters. The same could not be said about the red tank top and short denim overalls that she'd worn for painting on more than one occasion. "You see this?" She pointed to the cuff above her knee. "That's from my living room. And this spot up here…" She pointed to her chest. "This shade is in my bedroom."

Rad wished *he* was in her bedroom.

But she was in *his* bedroom. So was his bed. Yeah, it was covered with a drop cloth, but it was there, howling his name. He and Ben had carried it up early that morning. Serena was standing right beside it.

All it would take was a little maneuvering and presto, he could tumble her backward onto the wide mattress and have his way with her. The fit of his running shorts became tight as the mental images he was playing in his mind resembled something out of the Playboy Channel.

Oh yeah, he'd watch as Serena removed the backward baseball cap she had on her head, allowing her silky blond hair to tumble down over her shoulders. She'd slowly slide the strap of her overalls off one shoulder, then the other shoulder until the bib front fell to her waist, revealing her midriff tank top.

He had no idea if her tank top was midriff, but hey, this was *his* fantasy.

She'd give a seductive wiggle of her hips and shimmy out of her overalls, leaving her standing there in lacy-black underwear and a red tank top.

She'd come closer to him, sidling up to slide her hands up his arms, smiling her pleasure at the size of his biceps. He'd caught her eyeing him earlier, when he'd first changed into the ripped-off sleeveless black T-shirt that he used for workouts. Her hands would move beneath his shirt around his back. She'd run her fingertips over the ridges of his spine until they reached the elastic waistband of his running shorts. He closed his eyes with anticipation....

"Are you falling asleep?"

His eyes shot open to find Serena staring at him with concern rather than passion.

So much for X-rated fantasies. The woman of his dreams was standing there, showing no signs of starting any striptease routine.

"No, I was just thinking."

"About what?"

"About you."

She grinned at him. "Trying to figure out how I conned you into painting your bedroom Contentment Blue, huh?"

Trying to figure out how to coax you into my bed.

"You've gone awfully quiet all of a sudden," she noted. "Everything okay?"

"You're painting outside the lines."

"Excuse me?"

He pointed to the blue painters' tape he'd efficiently placed around the outlets, windows and woodwork. "Look, you've got paint on the plastic here. You're supposed to use the small brush or the foam brush for this detail work. Understood?"

"Aye, aye, mon capitain." Her salute was as saucy as her grin.

"What is that?" he demanded, irritated by the fact that she was in such a good mood when he didn't have her any closer to falling into his bed. "You think we're in the French Foreign Legion or something?"

"You know, I never noticed it before, but you're kind of cute when you get all grumpy like this."

Cute? *Cute?* Puppies and kittens were cute. Not Marines. Rad was speechless.

"Maybe it's the splatter of Contentment on your face." She reached up to touch his cheek.

He pressed her hand against the roughness of his skin before turning his head to kiss her fingertips. She shivered as his tongue darted out to brush the ultra-sensitive skin.

Serena raised her eyes to his. The undisguised passion she saw reflected there was almost her undoing.

Serena Sensual vs. Serena Serious. The wrestling match was intense. But somehow she found the willpower to lower her gaze and try to regain her composure. Serena Serious won this round. "We should get back to work. We still have another wall to paint yet."

"I'm hungry."

The way he said it, his voice all deep and rough and husky, made her melt all over again. And he spoke the words against her fingers, so she felt the words as well as heard them.

The fight wasn't over. This was only round two. Once again Serena Sensuous was duking it out with Serena Serious.

Her gaze darted over to the shrouded bed. She'd been aware of it since she'd walked into the room. It was hard not to, the thing was huge. King-sized at least, and the room wasn't all that big. She'd bumped into the bed more than once. Imagined him on it, naked, tangled in white sheets.

The struggle between her two halves intensified.

Then came the knockout punch. "I don't think I can wait," Rad murmured, nibbling at her fingertips. "How about you?"

Chapter Eight

Go for it. Take a chance. Grab what you want. Grab him!

Come on, an inner demon urged her. You've been bold before. You're an independent women. You can do this. Think how good it could be.

To which her sensible side said, Think of the heartache it could cause. It would forever change her relationship with Rad, ratcheting up the risk to an unacceptable level.

She just wasn't ready for that yet.

"I…can't," Serena stammered.

"Why not? Come on, you must be really hungry, too. Admit it."

Her voice evaporated. Even the little voices in her head fell silent, awed by the seductive pitch of Rad's delivery.

"We could share. Just tell me what you want."

Her tongue stuck to the roof of her mouth.

"Come on, you can tell me. Do you want it pure and simple or hot and spicy?"

The gleam in his brown eyes finally triggered a verbal response from her. "How do you like it?"

"With everything. The works."

"The works?"

"Oh, yeah. Extra mushrooms, sausage, black olives, pepperoni. That's the best way to have deep-dish pizza."

"Pizza?"

"Affirmative. Why?" He raised an eyebrow. "What did you think I was talking about?"

"You knew what I thought." She couldn't help herself, she had to sock him. He was a Marine, he could take it. "You did that on purpose."

"Did what?"

"Made me think you were talking about..."

"Yes?"

She wanted to sock him again, but all that had accomplished was making her even more aware of his powerful physique. Her fingers had practically bounced off his muscular arm. But the memory of touching his warm skin remained, stronger than ever.

She met the challenge she saw in his gaze. So, he thought she wouldn't say the word, did he?

Darn him, he was right.

She couldn't say sex, not when she was standing in Rad's bedroom with his ring around her neck. It was just all much too tempting. She needed a change of venue for this inner battle.

"Never mind. A pizza sounds good. But not in here.

The paint fumes will do us in." Hey, maybe that's why she was getting all weak-kneed and having these sexual fantasies. Paint fumes could be to blame. "Let's go downstairs to my place."

Rad agreed. "Sounds like a plan."

Serena wondered how her own plan to keep things between her and Rad strictly professional had gone so far astray. She also wondered what on earth she was going to do about it.

"Twenty bucks says the Bears whoop the Panthers." Rad peeled off the bill and placed it on the table of the sports bar where he and Ben were watching the *Monday Night Football* game on a big screen TV. They were seated in a corner, where Rad could see the entrance to the bar but had two walls at his back. Old habits died hard from his days as commander of a Scout-Sniper Platoon.

"You're on." Ben placed his twenty beneath the bowl of nachos. "They have zip pass protection. Easy pickings." Ben waited until the commercial to add, "So are you ready to tell me what's going on?"

"The Bears are behind by seven, but it's only the first quarter. There's a lot of football to be played yet."

"I meant with this fake engagement of yours. You told me to go along with whatever you said when you came to dinner the other night and I did. But now I want to know, what's the deal?"

Rad sighed and took a large swallow of his beer before replying. "The deal is that I needed to get a general's daughter off my back."

Ben lifted a brow. "You've been making out with a general's daughter?"

"No. General Burns's daughter had a thing for me. All I did was smile at her once and bang, she's in love with me."

"Yeah," Ben noted mockingly. "You've got that effect on women."

Rad tossed a nacho chip at him. "She's not a woman. Well, she is, but a very immature one. She's barely eighteen and spoiled by her daddy. She swore she'd make life difficult for me. That's when I decided to haul out a fictional fiancée."

"Serena?"

Rad nodded. "It seemed like a good idea at the time."

"It doesn't seem that way anymore?"

"It's getting much more complicated than I anticipated."

"No surprise there. So what made you pick Serena?"

"It was a fluke. Her name popped out of my mouth because I'd just met her earlier that day."

"And she agreed to pretend to be engaged to a man she barely knew? Why?"

"You don't have to know all the details. Look—" Rad pointed to the big screen TV "—the game's back on."

Ben waited until the next commercial before continuing his interrogation right where he'd left off. "So why'd she go along with such a stupid plan?"

"It's not stupid."

Ben just gave him a look.

"It's working," Rad maintained.

"Oh yeah? *Busha* told me about Heidi, the general's daughter, and how she had the hots for you. Doesn't sound like your engagement made that much of a difference."

Rad was appalled. "Great, now my grandmother is talking about my love life. As if I don't have enough problems."

"Why'd Serena say yes?"

"None of your business."

"You offered her money," Ben guessed.

Rad's expression darkened. "It wasn't like that."

"Then what was it like?"

"Look, she agreed to do me a favor."

"Out of the goodness of her heart? Come on, Rad. You're a Marine with loads of money. Women are gonna come after you. The twins have both already run into that situation."

"Serena did not come after me. This entire thing was my idea. She didn't even want me moving in upstairs."

"Upstairs from where?"

"Her apartment. She lives over the bookstore."

"Why did you move into her building?"

"It's not her building. It's my building. I bought it."

"When?"

"Recently."

"Ah."

"Ah what?"

"Now I get it." Before Rad could reply, Ben pointed to the big screen TV. "The game's on."

Rad tried not to grind his teeth. The fact that the Bears scored two touchdowns in the next ten minutes helped to mitigate his frustration with his brother. Of course it was Ben's duty as his brother to give him a hard time. That went with the territory. All the Kozlowski brothers knew that was a given. Brothers drove each other crazy and stood by one another, no matter what.

"No pass protection huh?" Rad tried not to gloat while a pair of twins with cheerleading pom-poms danced in a beer commercial on TV. "Back-to-back touchdowns."

"Remember when I whooped you at a game of darts?"

"You mean that one time over a year ago when I took pity on you and let you win because you were having women trouble?"

"I didn't have *women* trouble. There was only one woman in particular who was keeping me up nights. Both literally and figuratively."

"Yeah, I remember. You were falling for Ellie."

"Hard and fast. I recognize the symptoms, bro."

Rad's eyes widened and he put his hands up as if to ward off evil spirits. "You're way off base."

"Am I?"

"Absolutely."

"So you're not attracted to Serena?"

"Who wouldn't be? That makes me human, not infatuated."

Ben just shook his head. "I'm telling you, you've got it and you've got it bad."

"It?"

"Deny it all you want. I know what I saw when you looked at her all cow-eyed."

"You've been talking to Striker again."

Ben just grinned. "He'd tell you the same thing."

"That doesn't make it true. The game's on again." Rad watched the action on the football field, but his thoughts also remained on what Ben had said.

Love was not in his battle plan. He'd loved Liza, he

wasn't going through that again. Married-land was for his brother, not for him.

But Ben was right, things had changed. What had started out as a practical plan had turned into something more.

As often happened on the battlefield as new intel came in, Rad's mission changed. Success was still his goal. But instead of wanting Serena to pretend to be his fiancée, he wanted her…period.

And his new mission was to get her.

Rad was rather proud of himself. Sure it had taken him nearly two weeks, but he'd finally come up with something original, something that clearly pleased Serena. He'd invited her to one of the autumn festivals along the coast.

His mission to get Serena hadn't proved to be all that easy. She was obviously set on "caution mode." He'd taken her to dinner several times, and a movie once or twice, but she still held back.

He knew he had to move slowly so he wouldn't spook her, so he could prove he was nothing like her father, but he was getting impatient.

He'd managed to get past her defenses with some effective diversionary tactics and intel tactics. He'd found out from her assistant at the bookstore that Serena was a sucker for a festival.

Rad wasn't even sure what the event was, but when he'd mentioned it to Serena, her face had lit up and he'd wanted to kiss her. He'd wanted to do that, but he knew he had to proceed judiciously at this point. He had to woo her over to his way of thinking.

And okay, he'd be the first to admit that he was a little rusty in the wooing department. Normally women were readily available when he wanted one. He hadn't had to go after one since…Liza.

He shut down that train of thought and instead focused on Serena as they strolled around the festival grounds. She was wearing a short paisley skirt and a pink tank top. The weather was perfect for the third week in October, with blue Carolina skies and warm temps. Indian summer at its best.

Some sort of clip held Serena's long blond hair up. She was enjoying an ice cream cone filled with freshly made strawberry ice cream. The seductive lick of her tongue was enough to make his body throb. Pleasure was written all over her face.

The engagement ring he'd gotten her gleamed in the sunlight. He wasn't the only guy looking at her. But that ring proclaimed that she was his, that this female was taken.

Rad was a little surprised by his primitive reaction where Serena was concerned. He'd never been the jealous type before. If a woman was ready to move on, then so be it. He never got that involved. Not after Liza.

He wondered what she'd think of Serena. Outwardly the two were nothing alike. Liza had had dark hair and eyes. But they did share certain personality traits. They weren't easily taken in by surface charm; they tended to look for more depth.

The memory of Liza still haunted him, all these years later. He wasn't looking for that kind of heartache again. He wasn't looking for love with Serena, he was looking for…

A good time made it sound cheap and it wasn't true. He'd had good times before. He wanted more with her. That was the best way to put it. More. Not love. Just more.

He wasn't sure what Serena wanted, but it was his mission to make sure she wanted the same things he did. More.

"You want any more of that ice cream?" She was down to the last bite of the cone, and he hated to see the show end. He wanted to watch her tongue dancing over the pink creamy dessert. He really wanted her tongue dancing over him.

"Mmmm." She licked her lips. "That was delicious. But I shouldn't eat any more."

"Sure you should." *So I can see that tongue again.*

"No, I should show some restraint."

"No, you shouldn't. Restraint is highly overrated."

She raised an eyebrow at him. "This coming from a United States Marine? A man who cherishes order and detests chaos?"

"There's a time for restraint and a time for going all out, going for bust."

"Is that what you're doing today? Going for bust?"

Rad tried to keep his eyes off her bust but it was no easy task. The tank top showed off her breasts to perfection, allowing him to see just a hint of cleavage.

He tried to give her a Who-me? look.

She didn't look like she was buying it, but she didn't challenge him. Instead she said, "I find it hard to believe that you enjoy coming to a thing like this."

"You shouldn't. This event helps fund the Assembly Building that was used to assemble rockets during 'Operation Bumblebee' after World War II." He'd read that in a flyer they'd been given on their way in.

"So by being here, you're protecting an important part of military history. That makes sense then, I suppose."

"Haven't you ever wanted to do something that doesn't make sense?"

"Sure I have. More times than I can count."

"That's encouraging."

"I hardly think you need encouraging. You have enough confidence as it is."

"I'm still trying to recover from your harsh painting critique."

"I was not harsh. You're the one who gave me a hard time for painting outside the lines. I was merely being honest."

Not entirely true. If Serena had been totally honest she'd have told him how good he looked manning a roller brush. So many images of that day still remained so vivid in her mind—the ripple of his muscles, the surprising sexiness of his legs in those running shorts, the roughness of his skin as she'd touched his face with her fingertips.

That had turned out to be a wonderful day. Today was turning out to be another picture-perfect event.

She was having such a great time. Rad had been patient while she'd enjoyed the arts and crafts booths, even insisting on holding the small sunset photograph she'd bought from one of the artisans.

"Must be a sunset over the sound, huh?" he teased her, reminding her of their conversation that first night they'd gone out together.

That seemed like so long ago. So much had happened since then. So many things had changed.

Her feelings for him had grown. She'd tried hard not to let that happen but it had been impossible to fight. If he'd come on strong, if he'd pushed her, then she could have fought back. But Rad didn't do either of those things. Instead he went out of his way to make her feel special.

Like right now. He was holding her hand, his fingers intertwined with hers as if he wanted her to be a part of him.

"Are you getting hungry?" he asked.

His question reminded her of their conversation in his bedroom.

"What exactly did you have in mind?" This was something new for her, this ability to tease him, to flirt with him.

"Oh, I've got plenty of things in mind."

"I'm sure you do," she murmured.

"How about you?"

"How about me, what?"

"What did you have in mind?"

"Something hot and steamy...."

"Oh yeah."

"Does that sound good to you?"

Rad nodded.

She grinned. "Then let's head over to the Taste of Topsail section and see what trouble we can get into."

A variety of food vendors were set up along with picnic tables to enjoy their wares.

Ten minutes later, Serena was eating fried shrimp when she got some red shrimp sauce on her chin. Rad leaned forward, wiping the excess off with his thumb.

She gazed at him, awed by the power of his touch; such a simple thing creating such a complex reaction. For once she could read his thoughts in his eyes. He wanted to kiss her. He was *going* to kiss her. He took his time, leaning closer until his lips were almost brushing hers....

"Hi! Whatcha doin'?" Amy asked with the friendly interest of a six-year-old as she plunked down beside them on the picnic bench. "Were you gonna kiss her? Do you think cats kiss? I want a cat but I can't have one because of my asthma."

"I have two cats," Serena said, recovering quickly. "Bella and Oshi, a mom and a daughter."

Amy's face lit up. "Do you have any pictures of them?"

Serena shook her head. "Not with me, but I'll bring some next time I see you."

"There you are," Ellie said to her daughter. "I told you to stay close by."

"Yeah, but then I saw Uncle Rad." Amy rested her head on his shoulder and gazed up at him with a grin.

Ellie joined them on the picnic bench. "If I'd known you two were interested in coming here, I'd have included you in the invitation for the rest of the gang."

"What gang?"

"Wanda. Striker and his wife Kate and their baby son Sean. They flew in for the weekend. Didn't Ben tell you, Rad? I told him to tell you but he said you were busy."

Rad had been busy. Busy trying to seduce Serena. A minute later they were joined by the rest of the family. Introductions were made.

Striker was the oldest Kozlowski brother, the one who managed the family's oil business in Texas. He was smiling and at ease now, but Serena could tell this was a man who could keep secrets.

Ellie had told her that Striker was a former Force Recon Marine. His wife Kate had a classy elegance that could only come from being born into wealth. The smile the two shared told of their love, as did their affectionate attention to their son, sitting in a stroller and gurgling up at them with energetic waves of his little hands and that killer Kozlowski smile.

Seeing the family together, Serena couldn't help wondering what it would be like to have a child of her own. She hadn't wondered about that as much when she'd visited Ben and Ellie's house because Amy was older. And it wasn't just seeing a baby that did it. These thoughts hadn't occurred to her when her godchild Becky had been born ten years ago.

No, these thoughts were recent, coming to her in the past week or two. And they weren't just general musings, they were specific. Not what would it be like to have just any child of her own, but what would it be like to have *Rad's* child.

She'd tried to put the brakes on such fantasies. But they were incredibly powerful and gaining strength every day. It scared her, but at the same time it filled her with anticipation of what might happen next.

In the bookstore, she often talked about a compelling book—one that had her turning the pages quickly to read what was going to happen next. That's what her life felt like right now. Compelling. Forcing her to keep going to see what would happen next.

Serena tried to return to the present by making small-talk. "It's a beautiful day for this, isn't it?"

Wanda nodded. "October is one of my favorite months."

"Because it's Polish Heritage Month, right, *Busha?*" Ben teased her.

She smacked his arm affectionately. "Not just for that reason, but that is a good thing. October was chosen because it coincides with the death of the American Revolutionary War hero General Casimir Pulaski. Celebrating our heritage is something that should not be forgotten. It is up to us to instill Polish pride in the younger generation. If we don't do it, who will?" She turned to her oldest grandson. "Remember that, Striker, as you raise little Sean here. He comes from a proud heritage strong in family, faith and community."

"You could give any proud Texan a run for their money, right *Busha?*" Striker noted with a grin. "As proud as a pup with a new collar."

"That skunk ain't gonna mate," his wife Kate said. "That's Striker's favorite Texas saying because he made it up himself."

"It's sad to see what Texas has done to you," Rad noted with a regretful shake of his head.

"That dog won't hunt," Striker retorted.

"Another one of his favorites," Kate said.

"There are many wonderful Polish sayings as well. *Bez pracy nie ma kolaczy.* Roughly translated, that means Without work you won't get any cakes."

"Tell Ben that the next time he doesn't want to mow the lawn," Rad suggested to Ellie.

"Uncle Striker, will you tell daddy to put a miniature golf course in our backyard?" the ever-persistent Amy requested. "I can't drive yet, so I can't play whenever I want."

"Hey, want some cotton candy?" Striker said. The distracting question worked, as the two of them headed off to the vendor.

"She's a persistent little thing, isn't she?"

"Sometimes you have to be to get what you want," Ben noted with a tender look at Ellie. He paused for a quick kiss before adding, "Hey, has anyone heard from Mom and Dad?"

"We got a call right before we flew out here," Kate replied. "They seemed to be having a great time in New England. I meant to congratulate you earlier, Rad, on your engagement. *Busha* told me your good news."

"You didn't say anything to Mom and Dad about it, did you?" Rad demanded.

Kate shook her head.

"Good. I haven't had time to tell them yet."

Wanda frowned at him. "This is not a good thing to keep secret. Make time to speak to your parents."

"I will, *Busha*. But I want to do it my way."

"Oh, you." She socked his arm as she had his brother's earlier. "You always want to do things your way. And it is never an easy way."

"Marines aren't into easy," Ellie and Kate noted in unison before cracking up.

"Yeah, I'm learning that," Serena noted.

"I hope you don't mind my family butting in on our day together," Rad said as he and Serena walked along the beach later that evening.

"You have a nice family."

"They can be a little overwhelming en masse like that."

"That was only part of your family."

"I know. It's a real madhouse when everyone is around. Unfortunately it doesn't happen all that often, with our various schedules and deployments. So we enjoy the time we do have together."

"That sounds like a wise thing to do." She would love to just do that with Rad, simply enjoy the time they had together, not worry about the future, not worry that he was too much like her father. That had been her goal for today. To live in the moment.

"Looks like there might be a great sunset coming," Rad said. "Over the sound. Want to watch it?"

Serena nodded.

"There you go." Rad peeled off his denim shirt and laid it on the sand for her to sit on. That left him wearing a white T-shirt and jeans. He made a grand gesture, bowing as if he were some knight from one of those beautifully illustrated fairy tales she sold in her bookstore.

Taking his hand to steady herself, she sank onto the soft denim material. It was still warm from his body heat and the feel of that on her bare legs was somehow incredibly erotic.

Rad didn't sit beside her, but instead sat behind her, his splayed legs on either side of her body. "Just pretend I'm a chair," he told her. "Lean back against me."

There was no way she could imagine him as a piece of furniture but she did allow herself to rest against him. That allowed him to loosely wrap his arms around her waist and rest his chin on top of her head.

"There, isn't this a nice way to watch the sunset?" he murmured.

Nice didn't come close to describing what she was experiencing. In his arms she was a different person, forgetful of everything but the magic he created.

She turned her head and almost smacked his Adam's apple with her hair clip. "Sorry about that. I should take this out...."

"Allow me." He carefully removed the clip, his lean fingers creating dashes of fire wherever they touched on her scalp, then on her nape as he smoothed her hair as it tumbled down.

Yeah, being held by Rad was kind of like standing in the middle of a sunset. Basking in the glorious radiance, awed by the experience.

Shivers of pleasure raced through her as he played with a silky strand of her hair.

Rad brushed her bare arms with his large hands. "Are you cold? Here..." He bent his knees and leaned forward, effectively creating a warm hollow for her with his powerful body. "That better?"

She was surrounded by him. But instead of being overwhelmed by the experience, she was relishing it.

Clouds feathered across the sky, their presence adding to the show Mother Nature was staging for their benefit. Intense sunset colors were reflected in the water, creating a spectacular mirror image. The light fell in splashes: vivid yellow in the center with streaks of pink, crimson and indigo.

At the height of the chromatic display, Rad shifted her slightly in his arms and kissed her. Serena closed her eyes and gave herself over to the tender passion of his embrace. Unlike their previous sensual encounters, this time they lingered to enjoy the slightest of touches, to experiment with new angles of lips and mouths.

It was a Southern kiss, slow and hot, leisurely and luxurious. Not leading somewhere else, not angling for sex, but meant to be enjoyed for the journey itself and not the destination. For the first time since she'd met him, Serena stopped thinking and just let herself live in the moment.

One of her last coherent thoughts was that a girl sure could get used to this....

Chapter Nine

Two days later, Rad was leaving Serena's apartment in the early evening when he almost ran into someone—a female with short dark hair and suspicious eyes.

She looked him up and down before saying, "So you're the fake fiancé."

"So you're the college roommate," Rad replied, guessing that this had to be Lucy. Serena had told him that she'd confided in her best friend.

"I'm someone you do not want to upset. So don't do anything to hurt Serena."

Ben had told Rad how Ellie's friends had threatened him with bodily harm should he break Ellie's heart, but this was the first time Rad had experienced anything similar. Women had tended to throw themselves at him in the past, they'd been the ones to chase him. Sometimes he slowed down enough for one of them to catch him temporarily.

But none of them had ever sicced their friends on him.

Not that he really believed Serena had told Lucy to issue her warning. He had complete faith in Serena's ability to speak her own mind and fight her own battles.

Rad decided to turn the tables on Lucy. "Do you think Serena is stupid?"

"What? Of course not!"

"You don't trust her judgment?"

"Well, she does try to find the silver lining in bad situations."

"Looking for favorable outcomes is not a bad thing."

"I don't want anyone taking advantage of her."

"Neither do I. So we're on the same side on this. Allies."

He smiled at her before leaving.

Serena opened the door to find her friend standing there with a bemused look on her face. "I thought I heard voices out here."

"You did. I was talking to Bossy Marine Man."

"And how did that go?"

"He certainly has a way about him. Within two minutes he had turned things around so that he and I are allies in making sure no one takes advantage of you."

"I told you that he could be very convincing."

"No kidding. And very good-looking."

"I tried to warn you about that, too. But there's no way to prepare for one of his smiles. You don't see them coming, and wham, they hit you, making your tummy go all fluttery." Serena sounded dreamy.

Lucy frowned. "Yeah, but remember, this is the guy who scared Becky in school."

"He intimidated her, he didn't scare her. Rad has a

very powerful presence and that's what threw Becky. But I've seen him with his six-year-old niece Amy and he's incredibly good with her. He's good with his entire family. Well, I haven't actually met his entire family, just his grandmother and two of his four brothers and his two sisters-in-law and niece and baby nephew."

"He comes from a really big family, huh?"

"Yeah. All his brothers are Marines. Well, his older brother is in the reserves. Striker spends most of his time running King Oil in Texas these days."

"Marines with money." Lucy shook her head. "A rare thing indeed."

"The money is not the attraction." Serena tried not to sound too defensive.

"So you're admitting there is an attraction?"

"You saw him. He's an attractive guy."

"So this is just a physical thing?"

Serena sank down onto the couch with a sigh. "I wish it were that simple." That day spent at the autumn festival had marked a significant turning point in her relationship with Rad. She'd let her guard down and instead of bossing her, it was almost as if he were courting her. Not just trying to get her into his bed, but wooing her. Rad hadn't tried to rush her into something she wasn't ready for yet. Instead he'd seduced her with slow hot kisses in the sunset. Her toes curled with remembered pleasure.

Lucy joined her on the couch. "Are you sure you're not the one complicating things?"

"What do you mean?"

"Just that given your background, you have a track record of bailing on relationships before things get serious."

"This is different."

"Right. You told me this was supposed to be a simple business arrangement. But judging from the look on your face, there's nothing simple about it, is there?"

"No."

"So what are you saying? That you're falling for this guy? For real?"

"I could be." Even saying the words both scared and elated her.

"Which means you are. So what are you going to do about it?"

"I don't have a clue," Serena admitted, picking up one of the colorful throw pillows she'd made and hugging it against her tummy, which had gone all funny again.

"How does he feel about you?"

"We seem to share a pretty powerful chemistry between us."

"Chemistry? That's all?"

Serena shook her head. "What am I going to do?"

"Play it by ear. See how things go."

"What if I do fall for him even harder?"

"Would that be so awful?"

"He only started this fake engagement to get away from another woman."

"From a general's spoiled daughter. That's what you said, right? And how has that part of the story turned out?"

"I haven't seen Heidi lately. She dropped by the store once or twice in the beginning. Clay fell for her instantly."

"The poor guy."

"I know. She looked right through him. Sometimes

I think I catch something in her eye...loneliness or something. But then she says something outrageous that makes you want to smack her."

"Has she bought the story about your engagement to Rad?"

"She appears to have."

"But she hasn't backed off sufficiently for him to end the charade."

"No." Serena's stomach dropped at the realization that Rad could call things off at any time. Serena Serious put her foot down. "I shouldn't fall for him. It would be incredibly stupid. Not only is he totally wrong for me, but this whole thing is just make-believe."

Serena's attraction to Rad was in direct conflict to her vow never to be controlled again. Her aversion to bossy, military types hadn't disappeared.

While it was true that he wasn't as bad as her father, she couldn't kid herself into thinking that he was easy-going by any stretch of the imagination.

But when she was with Rad, she didn't think about any of those things.

Instead she was overcome by how great it felt to be with him, to watch how a rare smile took hold in his eyes before showing up on his sexy mouth.

She'd been experiencing all the classic signs associated with infatuation—nervousness, anticipation, accelerated heartbeats and that empty feeling that comes when you're not in their company.

But this was more than infatuation. This was big trouble.

"So tell me the silver lining," Lucy prompted her. "You can always find a silver lining."

"Well, I am finally getting my kitchen sink repaired."

"Is that why Bossy Marine Man was wearing that tool belt? Here I thought you two were into some kind of kinky role-playing sex game."

Serena reached forward to grab a *Publishers Weekly* magazine; one of the skinnier issues, off the coffee table and toss it at her. "You're bad, do you know that?"

"Of course I do. Now get out the chocolate and let's really talk."

Two hours later, Lucy had long since departed and Serena was enjoying the view of Rad stretched out on her kitchen floor, part of his upper torso hidden by the cabinet as he worked on the leaky plumbing. "So did your friend warn you off me?"

"What makes you think we were talking about you?"

"Weren't you?"

"Maybe. Briefly. Then we discussed my goddaughter's Halloween costume."

"Yeah, right."

"What? You don't believe me?"

"I find it hard to believe that a Halloween costume could be that fascinating."

"While you, on the other hand, are eminently fascinating, right?"

"You said it, not me."

"How did you learn how to do this kind of stuff anyway?"

"What kind of stuff? Being fascinating, you mean?"

"No. I mean this handyman kind of stuff."

"My dad. He felt all his sons should know the basics

of home repair so we could manage that stuff when he was deployed overseas."

"You must have moved around a lot."

"Yeah, but you know how that is."

She did. Staying just long enough to make friends only to pull up and move—having to start all over again. The most important thing she'd brought with her from place to place were her books. She'd left clothing behind to fit her books into the limited space her father had allowed her. "Four boxes, that's it. We can't be lugging junk all over. Show some discipline."

Rad's muttered curse returned her attention to the present. "Are you okay down there?"

"Just peachy."

"Did that connector you got at the hardware store work?" That's where he'd been headed when he'd run into Lucy outside Serena's apartment.

"Yeah, but the old one was a real dog to get off." She looked down at the play of muscles on his washboard abdomen as he wrestled with the plumbing. She was wrestling with Serena Sensuous again. It was so tempting to kneel down beside him and feel his warm skin. He'd removed his T-shirt earlier, baring his perfectly honed chest to her. The waistband of his jeans rested low on his hips, revealing his navel. Talk about prime masculinity poured into faded denim. Oh my....

Serena sank to the floor beside Rad. He was only inches away. It would be so easy to reach out and touch him, to trace her fingers over the ridges and planes of his abdomen.

Her gaze moved higher. The edge of his dog tags lay

between the silky-brown coins of his nipples. She wanted to lay her tongue against his flesh, to taste him, to lick him.

He shifted position so that less of his body was covered by the cabinet and more was displayed to her avid gaze.

How could she resist?

She had to do it.

She reached out...

"Hand me that wrench, would you?"

His words made her snatch her hand back, as if she'd almost gotten burned.

"Serena? The wrench?" He waggled his fingers.

She efficiently slapped the tool into his hand.

"Thanks."

"No problem." She had to keep talking or she'd jump him right there on her kitchen floor. "So your dad taught you all about home repairs, huh? Did he do other guy stuff, like teach you how to fish?"

"My Texas grandfather did that. That's one of the few things he taught me. We weren't very close. He didn't approve of my mom marrying a Marine named Kozlowski."

"I'm sorry to hear that."

"Yeah, well, that's life. Can you hand me some of that Teflon tape?"

"Sure."

"I told you that I fixed the front door to your apartment already, right? You don't have to worry about it not latching all the way now."

No, she only had to worry about falling in love with a tough Marine who had a body to die for.

* * *

"Your total is $30.08." Serena reached for a plastic bag while flashing the customer one of her best sales smiles. "Did you get a copy of our *Novel Newsletter?* It features upcoming events and new releases. No? Then I'll put in a copy for you. There you go." She handed over the bag and the woman's change. "I hope you enjoy your books."

Another smile, another customer.

And so it went for most of Saturday, their busiest day of the week. Business was unusually brisk today.

Which was why Serena was especially glad when Kalinda finally arrived.

"Sorry I'm late. Where's Clay? I called him to come cover for me until I got here."

"He's in the back room, unpacking the latest order shipments."

Serena could tell by Kalinda's strained expression that something was wrong, but there was no time to ask her about it as a steady stream of customers kept them both busy.

Finally, a little after four, there was a lull in the traffic. "Everything okay?" Serena asked.

"No. It's my father again. He's driving me crazy."

"What's the matter?"

"The same old thing." Kalinda sipped the cappuccino she'd made earlier, but hadn't had a chance to drink much of yet. "He only wants me dating Indian boys. I thought I'd finally come up with the perfect plan— going out with an Indian boy who's a friend of mine, nothing romantic, and then hooking up with my real date. But that backfired when the platonic guy suddenly started getting ideas despite the fact that he'd agreed to the entire thing beforehand."

"Uh-oh."

"Yeah. Major bummer. You know, it's not that I'm not proud of my Indian culture. I am. And when Wanda comes in and tells me about her Polish heritage, I tell her about my heritage. We've even exchanged recipes. She gave me one for *kolachkis* and I gave her one for *kheer*. She's told me about Dyngus Day and I told her about Diwali."

Serena wondered how she could have missed all this going on. Oh, she realized that Wanda often stopped by, but she hadn't realized how close Kalinda and the older woman had become. But then Serena had been consumed by her own situation with Rad.

"Diwali is the Festival of Lights, right?" At least Serena knew something. She remembered Kalinda had told her about it last year.

"That's right. It's going on now and it's the one Hindu festival that unites all of India. It's also celebrated by Indians all over the world. We light small oil lamps called *diyas* and place them around our homes and gardens. Candles can be substituted for *diyas*. The celebrations include exchanging special sweets and gifts and then ends in fireworks. Diwali is meant to be an occasion for cheerfulness and togetherness. But the only fireworks at my house this year are between my father and me."

"Does he know about you using your Indian friend as a cover for going out with someone else?"

"He suspects. That's what we were arguing about before I left for work."

"Do you want to go home and talk…?"

"Why? My father is much too stubborn to listen to me. And my mother is no help."

Serena could relate.

"They just don't understand me."

Again, Serena could empathize.

"I only want a little freedom. That doesn't seem like much to ask, does it?"

Serena shook her head.

"Anyway, Wanda has been really cool about all this heritage sharing stuff. It's kind of cosmic that October is both Polish Heritage Month and it's also usually the month we celebrate Diwali. India has a solar calendar so the date varies each year, but it's always late fall."

"Have you talked to Wanda about your dad?"

"No, not really. I figured she'd be into obeying parents and all that. Listen, let's change the subject, okay?" Kalinda tucked her long black hair behind her ears and smiled, albeit half-heartedly. "Hey, have you noticed that Clay seems a lot happier lately?"

"I had noticed that, yes." When Serena had asked him to work on the incoming shipments in the back, he'd offered to do some additional computer work while he was there. Clay was a good part-timer, but he rarely offered to do extra work in the past.

"Given that Clay is often in a world of his own, it's sometimes hard to tell how he's feeling, but he actually smiled at me yesterday." Kalinda shook her head as if still surprised by the memory. "I think he's met someone."

"Someone?"

"A girl."

"Has he said anything to you?" Serena asked her.

"Are you kidding? Clay never talks about his private life."

"Like another guy I know," Serena muttered.

"You mean Rad?"

Serena nodded. "I still don't know what he does in the Marine Corps. I mean, I know he's a Captain. But I don't know what he does."

"Maybe it's something top secret."

"His grandmother told me that she thinks he's saving the world from evil."

Kalinda grinned. "Well then, that explains it. Does it really matter what he does?"

"He knows so much about my work, it would be nice to know something about his. A way of sharing."

"You should be thankful he doesn't talk about work all the time. My father does that. He's an anesthesiologist you know, and he's always talking about some patient. And he always does it while I'm trying to eat. It's gross. I've told him so, but he doesn't care. He's the father." Kalinda used her hands to place quote marks around her words. "He's all knowing."

"Kinda like my Mystical Magic Ball," Clay noted, having walked in on the tail end of the conversation.

Kalinda leaned over the counter to get a better view. "Where did you get that?"

"A friend gave it to me."

"I don't know. It seems pretty simplistic for a techie like you," Kalinda teased him.

"Let's see what it says." Clay turned it upside down. "What do you want to ask it?"

She immediately replied, "Will Kalinda outwit her father?"

"The outcome is too cloudy to predict," Clay read.

"Ask it something about Serena." Kalinda nodded toward her.

"Like what?"

"How about if the after-school program on Tuesday will go off okay?" Serena had arranged for drama students from the local high school to read aloud to at-risk kids. It was part of her overall strategy for the store—to make books come alive. She knew from her own experience that once you hooked a kid on reading, they're usually hooked for life.

Clay turned over the ball and read, "Very likely."

Kalinda shared a high-five with Serena. "Ask if she'll keep getting flowers from her fiancé." Rad had been sending them like clockwork every week. "And that yummy imported dark chocolate."

"Most likely."

Kalinda continued with her questions. "Ask it if I'll get an A in my Advanced Calculus class."

"Most likely."

"Yes!" Kalinda did a little happy dance before saying, "Ask it if Serena and Rad will live happily ever after."

"The outcome is too cloudy to predict," Clay reluctantly read.

Yeah, that's what Serena was afraid of.

"I think I'm finally getting the hang of this." Serena smiled as Rad put a hand under her elbow to help her out of his Corvette. He had on a pair of charcoal-gray pants paired with a crisp white shirt and he looked good enough to eat.

But she was struck by more than just his good looks. She loved the way he made her feel all feminine and cherished by doing little things like opening doors for her. Rad didn't do it as a way of controlling her, but as a way of showing her respect. The old-fashioned chivalry was incredibly endearing.

"What do you mean you're getting the hang of this?"

She smoothed the jersey of her black dress. "I mean I think I've finally mastered the art of getting out of a low-slung sports car without making a fool of myself."

"I have yet to see you make a fool of yourself. I, on the other hand, have done so several times."

"Name one."

"When you walked in on me lying spread-eagle on your living room floor yesterday."

She grinned. "That was sweet, not foolish." He'd been trying to coax her cats to come out from beneath the end table. It wasn't the first time he'd tried to befriend them, but on that occasion he'd used the right bait—a fluffy pink feather toy with a long stick. That way he could lie in wait, getting down to their level so he didn't tower over them.

Oshi had remained cautious, but Bella had gone for the toy.

Rad's grin of satisfaction had been Serena's downfall. She'd known then and there that she was in love with him. It was no longer a matter of falling in love, she was already there.

Since this revelation had come less than twenty-four hours ago, Serena still wasn't sure what to do about it. Her concerns remained. And Rad hadn't expressed his feelings for her.

But for now she resolved to live in the moment and just enjoy this evening.

More than one female head turned as they walked into the cozy harborside Italian restaurant. They'd come to Cacino Italia to meet Rad's grandmother and Striker and Kate for dinner.

"Do you realize what's coming up next week?" Rad asked her as they waited to be seated.

"Yes. Halloween. And the *Harry Potter* party at the store."

"I was referring to our one-month anniversary. We'll have to do something special to mark the occasion."

Before Serena could react to his comment, the hostess gestured them to her side. "If you'll follow me, please."

Serena was very aware of Rad's splayed fingers on her back as the hostess led them toward the back of the large restaurant. She was also aware of the fact that he'd taken note of their one-month anniversary. What did that mean? That he was too aware of the time dragging out? Or that he enjoyed every moment? Or someplace in between?

What did doing something special mean? Ordering another deep-dish pizza together? Making love? What?

She was so distracted by her thoughts that she didn't even register the fact that they'd stepped into a very dimly lit room. It wasn't until the lights were suddenly turned on and a crowd of people shouted "Surprise!" that she realized what had happened.

For one second Serena thought they must have walked into the wrong room.

Then she looked around and recognized the people standing around her.

But the biggest shock of all was caused by the two people who stayed apart from the rest. Two people she hadn't seen in years, two people who were supposed to be a thousand miles away in Nevada, not here in North Carolina.

Her parents.

Chapter Ten

"Are you surprised?" Heidi asked Rad, taking him by the arm and drawing him aside.

"Affirmative." His voice was curt. "Especially given the fact that I specifically told you that I didn't want you throwing a party for us."

Heidi waved his words away. "Like what girl wouldn't love a surprise engagement party?"

This girl, Serena wanted to shout.

The dream world she'd been allowing herself to believe in was quickly coming unraveled. Reality was staring her in the face. Her *father* was staring her in the face. And she could tell he wasn't happy with what he saw.

But then he rarely was. Not when he looked at her.

Can't you do anything right? What were you thinking? You always were a troublemaker. Up to no good. Wild. Undisciplined. Trouble.

She'd heard the accusations so many times. Seen the look of disappointment. Heard the anger.

Serena Sunshine tried to find a silver lining here... but it was tough.

Maybe her father had mellowed over time.

Oh yeah? an inner voice taunted. You mean since last Christmas when he'd said you'd never amount to much and that opening a bookstore was the stupidest idea he'd ever heard of?

So much for her spirit-of-the-holiday-inspired idea of calling her parents last December to mend bridges.

Why were they here? Why had they come from Las Vegas instead of refusing? How had Heidi known how to contact them?

Serena had no answers. Instead she was filled with millions of questions and lots of dread.

"Looks like Serena has finally done something right," her dad was telling Striker. "Getting herself hooked up with a jarhead. Maybe he'll knock some sense into her. She was a total screwup, you know. I never could get her to toe the line. Your brother is going to have his hands full with this one, I can tell you."

Serena stood there frozen, unable to think of a way to make this nightmare stop.

Striker did his part by walking away as quickly as he could. Which meant what? That he was disgusted with her father, or with her?

As the minutes slowly ticked by, things got worse. Her father always had had a booming voice, and it carried in the room despite the other conversations flowing on around him.

Looking at the large framed photographs of Rome and

Venice decorating the walls, Serena desperately wished she could crawl into one of them and just disappear.

Serena jumped when someone touched her arm. "Are you okay?" Ellie asked her. "You look a little pale. Actually you've got a definite deer-in-the-headlights look."

Serena grabbed Ellie as if she were a lifeline. "Listen to me, don't let Wanda talk to my parents. Keep her away from them."

Ellie nodded with the air of one who recognized sheer panic. "Okay. No easy task, but I'll do my best."

All Serena needed was for Wanda to ask her mom about her Polish heritage. Or for Wanda to hear about any of her escapades from her father.

The house of cards she and Rad had built was now precariously perched on the edge of a fault zone and the earthquake was only a matter of time.

Where was Rad? He'd left her side to go talk to his brother Ben. Maybe he was ordering him to clear the room?

"I can't believe you let them do this." Rad glared at Ben. "Whatever happened to watching my back? Leave no man behind, remember?"

"Listen, I was totally out of the loop. Ellie didn't tell me what was going on until we got here about five minutes ago. I tried to call you but your cell phone was off."

"What about Striker?"

"What about him?" Ben kept his voice low. "He doesn't know that your engagement isn't the real thing—unless you've told him?"

Rad shook his head. "The more people who know that piece of intel, the more likely the word will get out."

"Agreed. Just consider yourself lucky that Mom and Dad couldn't get here in time. Their RV broke down in some remote place in Maine so they were stuck there."

"But Serena's parents are here."

"Yeah."

Rad looked across the room, his attention focused on her father. This was the man who'd made Serena so gun-shy about military men. He was average height and above-average width, the beginning of a beer belly stretching the material of his shirt. He had sandy hair and eyebrows and the look of a man who spent a lot of time out in the sun. And he had a wife who was gazing at him anxiously, but not doing anything to keep him quiet—unless you counted those nervous little touches to the arm that were clearly being ignored by the big guy.

He noticed that Serena had yet to actually greet them. But it didn't look like that could be put off any longer. Her father was on the move.

Rad left his brother to return to Serena's side for backup support. If there were any battles to be fought, he wasn't about to let her fight them alone.

Serena spoke first. "Mom, Dad." She smiled and nodded at them both. They nodded back. "I'm surprised to see you here."

Her father did all the talking. "We were surprised to hear you got engaged without talking to us first. Not that we should have been. You never tell us what you're doing until you've already done it and made a mess of things." Frank turned his attention to Rad. "Since she didn't bother to introduce us, I'll do it myself. I'm Frank Anderson and this is my wife Iris. As I was telling your brother Striker earlier, I'm glad to see Serena here has hooked up with a jarhead. Maybe you can get her to toe the line. I sure never could."

Rad took Serena's hand in his. Her fingers were ice cold. "I don't need anyone telling me to toe the line," Serena stated.

"Sure you do," Frank said. "To keep you out of trouble."

"If you'll excuse us, I see someone we need to speak to." Rad efficiently whisked Serena away to the far corner of the room. Or he tried to, but they were stopped several times by well-wishers.

"I had no idea Heidi was going to pull a stunt like this," Rad assured Serena once he had her in a relatively quiet corner. "I told her not to."

"And we can see how well she obeyed that order." Serena's voice was tart.

"This isn't my fault."

But she wasn't listening to him. All she could hear was her father's voice from the other side of the room.

No, it wasn't Rad's fault that her parents had shown up tonight. It wasn't his fault that her father couldn't seem to accept her for who she was. It wasn't his fault that the age-old hurt and resentment from her childhood was coming back with a vengeance.

She was an adult now. She should be able to handle situations like this. "How did Heidi get all these people here?"

"I don't know, but I plan on finding out."

"Not now." She grabbed his arm. "Don't make a scene now." Her father was doing that on his own, she didn't need to add more fuel to the fire.

"Okay."

Serena stuck it out, the smile she used to placate difficult customers plastered to her face, for as long as she could. But the humiliation was growing by the second.

Then she heard it, the words she'd been dreading all night.

"There's nothing wrong with being rebellious," Striker's wife Kate said, defending Serena. "I wish I'd been more rebellious as a teenager."

"Serena was more than rebellious. She was a regular juvenile delinquent. She was arrested for theft, you know," her father declared in that booming voice of his.

All conversation in the room ceased.

Serena had had enough. She couldn't breathe. "I can't do this!"

She had to get *out!* She ran to the nearest exit, not caring that it was an emergency exit and that the alarms went off as she left.

By the time Rad made his way through the chaotic crowd and got outside, Serena had disappeared.

A moment later, Frank joined him, shaking his head. "She's up to her old tricks again. Disappearing when the going gets tough."

Wanda put a restraining hand on Rad's arm, as if sensing that Rad was just itching to deck the older man and that only years of Marine Corps training was keeping his anger under wraps.

"You should not be insulting my grandson's fiancée the way you have been doing. That is very wrong of you." Wanda shook a finger at Frank. "You have no idea how lucky you are to have a daughter like Serena.

Someone so clever and hardworking. So kind and generous. A real man would be proud of such a daughter!"

Deciding his grandmother could take care of giving Frank the business, Rad concentrated his efforts at looking for Serena. He checked the parking lot, the businesses next door, but there was no sign of her.

Serena didn't stop running until a stitch in her side proved to be too painful to ignore any longer. Somehow she'd ended up several blocks away from the restaurant, on the beach, the sand pouring into her strappy sandals. Leaning over to catch her breath, she kicked her shoes off.

The rhythmic sound of the ocean soothed her battered soul. It was amazing how much words could hurt. They left bruises as surely as physical blows.

She'd never been sure why her father couldn't love her. He had once. She remembered being cuddled as a little kid, remembered him smiling at her and calling her his pumpkin. But once she'd gotten older and had started questioning his orders, things had changed.

The harder he'd been on her, the more she'd acted out, starting a destructive cycle that hadn't ended until the night she'd graduated from high school and taken his car without permission.

She'd lied and told her mother that he'd said it was okay. It was a lie that would cost her dearly.

Her father had reported the car stolen.

The police found her at three in the morning. She could still remember how terrified she'd been at seeing the flashing lights of the squad car in the Ford's rearview mirror.

She'd tried to explain that she wasn't a thief, that the car belonged to her father. The burly cop hadn't cared.

He'd placed her in the back of the cruiser as if she were a common criminal. She'd been fingerprinted and interrogated.

"This is all a mistake," she'd kept telling them. "A big mistake."

"It's a big mistake, all right." The cop had looked down at her sternly. "A big mistake you made, young lady."

She'd gotten one phone call. She'd called home. Her father had answered. She'd tried not to cry as she'd told him where she was.

"I know," he'd said. "Maybe this will teach you a lesson."

It had.

Serena sat on the beach, her position the same one she'd adopted that night she'd spent in lockup—her bent knees locked to her chest, her arms tightly wrapped around them as she tried to make herself as small and inconspicuous as possible.

The moon came out from behind a cloud, shimmering down on the waves rolling onto the beach. A sea breeze ruffled her hair. She reached up to touch her face, surprised to feel a tear rolling down her cheek.

That night had changed everything for her. She'd no longer hoped for the best. She'd expected the worst. At least where her parents were concerned. And she'd left her father's house. He'd kicked her out, but leaving immediately was the one thing they'd both agreed on.

She'd packed up the four boxes she'd always had to fit her belongings into for every move and had gone to a girlfriend's house for a few days. Since Serena had already been accepted at UNCW, she'd simply gone to Wilmington early.

It had been hard at first, but she'd managed, getting a job as a waitress, moving in with three other girls for the summer until her dorm room was available.

That had been eleven years ago, but some wounds didn't disappear with time.

Oh, they healed over, but the scab remained. And tonight's debacle had brought it all back with a vengeance.

She wiped her tears away but they kept silently coming, slowly but consistently.

Her engagement ring glowed in the moonlight. Rad wouldn't want to continue the charade any longer, not now that he'd met her father and heard about her past. His fellow Marines had been there as well, men he worked with. Now they all knew that she wasn't the sedate bookseller she'd worked so hard to become.

Humiliation washed over her as surely as the waves hitting the shore. Her father's cruel barbs were impaled deep within her. Maybe this pain was the price she had to pay for her sins of the past.

Lucy knew her history. Lucy would understand. Serena reached for her cell phone and dialed her best friend's number, then belatedly remembered that she and her family had gone down to Disney World for ten days. But before she could disconnect, someone answered. It was Lucy's twenty-four-year-old younger brother Bobby, who was house- and pet-sitting. "Hey, Serena, howyadoin?"

"Any chance you could come give me a lift?" she asked in a wobbly voice.

He was there within minutes. By then Serena had text messaged Rad to let him know that she was okay and not to come after her tonight. She'd had all the upheaval she could handle for one evening.

"That future father-in-law of yours is some piece of work," Striker noted.

"Yeah." Rad couldn't concentrate. He just needed to know Serena was okay.

"We could start a search party and go after her," Striker suggested.

It's what Rad wanted to do. But he suspected Serena would hate that, being tracked like an enemy combatant. "No."

"Your wife is looking for you," Ben told Striker as he joined them. He waited until he and Rad were alone before speaking again. "What are you going to do now?"

Rad looked down at his cell phone and the text message he'd just this moment received from Serena. As difficult as it was, he had to go against his natural instinct to confirm for himself that she was okay.

She didn't want to see him.

He couldn't blame her.

"Serena was never comfortable with any of this, you know." Rad's voice was flat. "She didn't like the deception. I practically had to force her to do what I wanted. She accused me of being like her father, but I didn't get it. Not until tonight. Now I understand what she meant."

"There's no way you're like him."

"Think about it. He wanted her to be obedient, to do what he wanted."

"Most guys feel that way at one time or another."

"Yeah, but most of them don't act on it. They don't create situations where the other party has no choice. At least, *real* men don't do that."

"You didn't blackmail her into saying yes."

"I might as well have. I knew she was in tough financial straits. So I made her an offer she couldn't refuse."

"I repeat, what are you going to do now?"

"I'm going to make it right."

"How are you going to do that?"

After Rad observed her father complaining about his daughter and how headstrong and difficult she'd always been, he finally understood what Serena had told him before. *He didn't hit me with his fists. His words were as powerful as a punch.*

"She told me how she hated being bossed around. I could see how important freedom of choice was to her. But by arm-twisting her into this fake engagement, I took that away from her. In the very beginning, I made a big deal out of telling myself that marriage wasn't for me, how I wasn't giving up my freedom. I valued it. But I didn't value Serena's freedom. The freedom to make her own choices was as important to Serena as the Marine Corps values of honor, courage and commitment are to me."

"Talk to her."

Rad nodded, but he already knew that there was only one thing to be done. Rad had to put things right for her, no matter what the cost.

When Serena entered her apartment later she saw the light blinking on her answering machine. Bella ran to greet her and started purring. Picking up the small cat, she cradled it against her chest and rubbed her face against the plush gray fur.

Bella's purr got even louder.

Here was unconditional love.

The moment was interrupted by the sound of pounding on her door. Bella flew out of her arms and headed under the couch. Serena wished she could join her.

But there was no point putting off the inevitable. She might as well face the music. She opened the door, expecting to see Rad. Instead she found her parents standing there.

"We need to talk." Her mother's voice was so uncharacteristically emphatic that Serena was momentarily stunned.

Iris walked into the apartment with her husband in tow.

"I think I've already heard enough about how difficult I am for one evening," Serena wearily noted.

"You should have told us you were engaged," her father said.

"You should have told the police that I didn't steal your car," Serena shot back, that devastating moment still fresh in her mind thanks to his comments this evening.

"I wanted to teach you a lesson."

"What lesson? That you didn't love me? Believe me, I already knew that."

"Sure," he growled, "blame me for all your mistakes."

"That's enough, Frank," her mother said.

Her sharp voice had both Serena and her father staring at her in amazement.

Squaring her shoulders, Iris seemed to grow in stature before Serena's eyes. "This has gone on long enough." Iris faced her husband, her gaze direct. "I will not allow you to ruin Serena's happiness. I've stood quietly by for far too long. I can't change the past, but I can prevent history from repeating itself. Enough is enough. Either you shape up, Frank, or I'm leaving you."

Frank was stunned. "You...you've never spoken to me like that before," he sputtered in disbelief.

"Maybe I should have. I love you, Frank, but there are times when you can be a donkey's behind. I haven't stayed with you all these years because you made me. I did it because I love you. Now you be a man about it. Look your daughter in the eye." She turned him to face Serena. "See the pain that you've caused her and then swear you won't hurt her again, that you're going to honor her choices. Tell her that you love her."

It was a life-altering moment for them all. Serena froze, unable to believe this was really happening.

She wanted to swing away from her father's inspection, but couldn't—not given her mother's astounding burst of courage. So Serena met her father's gaze head-on. At first she hid her pain beneath the cloak of resentment and rebellion that she'd used to hide her emotions since her adolescent years. But then she recognized her old patterns for what they were.

Despite the huge emotional risk, she let some of the rejection and pain show through.

Frank looked into his daughter's eyes and slowly his expression changed. The stubbornness and hardness fell away as he finally saw the damage he'd done.

Serena saw something flicker in his green eyes, so like her own. It was a combination of things she'd never seen before.

Vulnerability.

Regret.

Sorrow.

In the end all Frank could say was "I'm sorry" before his voice broke and he uncertainly held out his arms.

Serena took one hesitant step forward, then another.

Her father met her more than halfway, taking her in his arms for a bear hug like he used to give her as a child.

Serena had been so consumed by the painful moments in her past that she'd almost forgotten the good ones. She'd briefly remembered them on the beach earlier that evening, but only in comparison to her father's later behavior.

Now she closed her eyes, inhaled the smell of Old Spice and allowed the good memories to return....

Like the time her father had taken her to a football game and let her sit on his lap because she was too small to see over the heads of the other people. He'd gotten her a hot dog and hadn't complained when she'd gotten mustard all over herself and him.

He'd taken her trick-or-treating, come to father-daughter night at the middle school she'd just entered, painted her pink with Calamine lotion when she'd gotten chicken pox at age eight.

They'd gotten far off track, but Serena suddenly had a flicker of hope that with help and time, they could find their way back.

It was a start. A milestone, really. She didn't think she'd ever heard her father apologize for anything before in her entire life. And she'd certainly never seen her mother become so assertive.

This was all new territory, but it felt like one filled with hope and possibilities.

When her parents left a short while later, with the promise to meet again for breakfast, Serena felt at peace for the first time in years.

But that newfound serenity was shattered moments later when she played the single message on her answering machine.

Chapter Eleven

Rad's expressive voice filled the room as it floated up
from the tiny answering machine speaker. *I'm sorry I
dragged you into this mess of an engagement, but you
don't have to worry about it any longer. I'm calling it
off and setting you free.*

Rad was calling off the engagement! The words all
blurred together as Serena's knees gave way and she
sank onto a dining-room chair.

Serena was devastated. Had her father's talk about
her wild past and arrest made Rad ashamed of her? Was
he breaking off their engagement because of that? Because she was no longer suitable, even as a fictional fiancée?

The old Serena would have taken her pain and angrily shoved it deep down inside. But the new Serena
examined her emotions and Rad's. She'd just been

through an epiphany with her parents. She wasn't going to jump to conclusions here.

What's not to get? Serena Serious demanded. It's over.

He didn't say that, Serena Sensuous denied. There's something else going on here.

What *exactly* had he said? Every word mattered now. She was searching for clues.

She played the message again, this time noting his voice when he talked about setting her free. His inflection was definitely on the word *free*, along with comment about her not worrying anymore.

Which meant what?

Bella popped her head out from beneath the couch, cautiously checking to see if the coast was clear. Once she'd assured herself it was, she strolled out as if she hadn't just been spooked. Her recovery time really was remarkable.

Serena needed to take a page out of Bella's book.

The cat jumped up on Serena's lap before curling up and starting to purr. Within sixty seconds Oshi had joined her.

The image of Rad, laid out on her dining-room floor trying to coax the cats to play, to trust him, came vividly to mind.

Serena reviewed what she knew—that she loved him. That he seemed eager to reassure her that she was free. That maybe he finally understood how important freedom was to her, now that she valued love more.

Okay, there was only one thing to be done here. She loved Rad. She needed to take action.

"I'm not letting him go without a fight!" Saying the

words aloud made them seem more powerful. After the breakthrough she'd had with her father, she had to believe that anything was possible. Coming to terms with her past gave her the courage to go after him.

"Right, girls?" Okay, so a part of her was still nervous enough to check with her cats. Her version of Clay's Mystical Magic Ball. Oshi and Bella gazed up at her. "Blink once if you agree with me."

They did.

Not that Serena would have abandoned her plans if they hadn't, but still it was nice to get a sign, even one as lame as a feline blink.

"Good girls." She rubbed a cat with each hand, focusing on the spot behind their ears that was a favorite of theirs.

A moment later, a knock on the door startled them all.

Rad?

The cats flew off into the bedroom while Serena flew to the door, too excited to even remember to check the peephole before opening the door.

Heidi stood there.

Serena's stomach dropped to the other side of the universe. "Haven't you created enough trouble for one night?"

"I'm so sorry." Heidi's voice caught. "I didn't mean for things to get out of control. And now Clay isn't speaking to me. You have to help me."

"Clay?"

Heidi nodded. "Don't fire him. It was my fault. I told him that I was throwing a surprise party and that's why he gave me your parents contact info. He accessed your computer files."

"My private address book."

Heidi nodded and did look truly remorseful. In fact, she looked messy, not her usual glam self at all. Tears were running down her face and her mascara was smeared.

"Please don't fire Clay. He really needs this job and he loves working for you."

"I won't fire Clay."

"Thank you so much." Heidi then burst into tears.

"Why are you so upset?"

"My father would be so ashamed of me."

"Are you afraid I'm going to tell him? Is that why you're crying?"

Heidi hiccuped. "My dad doesn't care what I do. He only cares about the Marine Corps."

Serena handed her a tissue. "He cared enough to intervene on your behalf when you wanted Rad's attention."

"He was just doing that to like placate me, you know? He doesn't really *see* me."

Serena certainly knew firsthand how tenuous father-daughter relationships could be, filled with intricate and contradictory feelings…all intertwined together.

"And now Clay is furious with me," Heidi continued.

"Why do you care?"

"Because I like him. I really like him." Heidi gazed at Serena as if she held the answers to the world's deepest mysteries. "What can I do to make things up with him?"

"You and Clay? You have to admit, you're an unlikely pair."

"You mean because he's so smart?"

"I mean because you two don't seem to have anything in common."

"He treats me, like, with so much respect." Heidi's voice reflected her awe and her expression was positively dreamy. "I never had anyone treat me that way before. As if what I think matters and like not just the way I look."

Serena couldn't help wondering if this was some new ploy by Heidi, if the teenager had something new up her sleeve. But then she saw the pain in Heidi's eyes and she realized that Heidi did truly have feelings for Clay.

"You have to let him know how you feel. You have to talk to him and make him listen."

After Heidi had apologized again and thanked her profusely, Serena closed the door and reminded herself to take her own advice. She had to talk to Rad, to make him listen. The question was how…?

Mondays were usually catch-up days when Serena did the million-and-one things that needed to be done since the store was closed that day. The breakfast with her parents had gone well.

But now Serena had to concentrate on Rad.

She'd called his cell number and gotten his voice mail. She'd been up half the night planning what to say. None of it could be said over the phone. Except for this much—

"Rad, it's Serena. I *need* you to come over to my place tonight because something critical is broken in my apartment. I'll be waiting for you."

Serena jumped as the phone rang a moment later.

"Rad?"

"No, it's Kalinda. I was just calling to see how you are?"

"I'm okay."

"I have to tell you, after meeting your dad at that party last night, suddenly mine doesn't look so bad anymore. I had to leave early and go home and talk to him. It went well."

"Actually both my parents came over to my apartment last night and we…well, we made some real breakthroughs."

"That's good."

"Listen Kalinda, I've got to go. There's someone at my door."

She hung up and grabbed the doorknob, checking the peephole this time as she undid the dead bolt. Clay stood there, looking incredibly nervous.

She opened the door.

Before she could say a word, he launched into a speech. "I'm sorry to bother you at home and all that, but this can't wait. I probably should have just told you on the phone, but I figured I owed you a face-to-face meeting. I'm going to quit so you don't have to fire me. I know what I did was stupid and wrong."

Serena nodded. "It was. But I already told Heidi I wasn't going to fire you."

"When?"

"When she came to my apartment last night."

"I'm sorry she bothered you," Clay said, looking miserable.

"I think she really cares about you, Clay. I think she made a big mistake and that she regrets it."

"She used me to get what she wanted, which was to throw that party. I had no idea that you guys didn't want it to happen. She acted like it was all a special plan and everyone would be cool with it. She handled everything. All I had to do was get the information from your personal address book on your hard drive. She picked who was invited. I'm not good at social stuff like that."

"Heidi took all the blame when she spoke to me. She also told me that she thinks you're pretty special."

"Yeah, when I can get her info she wants," Clay noted morosely. "She's left me a bunch of messages, but I didn't listen to any of them."

"At least listen to what she has to say. People make mistakes. That's life. It doesn't mean you give up."

Serena reminded herself of that fact as she waited the rest of the day for Rad to appear.

"Thank you for meeting me for lunch today," Wanda told Rad as they sat down at a fast-food place near the base.

"You weren't taking no for an answer."

Wanda nodded her agreement with his observation and took the salad he handed her. "Ellie let me borrow her minivan to come here today."

"So what is so important?"

"You are."

"What about me?"

"There's a Polish proverb that goes something like this—*love enters a man through his eyes, a woman through her ears.*"

"Which means what?" Rad couldn't help being impatient. He'd hadn't gotten much sleep last night.

"That you have to tell Serena how you feel."

"I already told her that she's free." The only contact he'd had with her since then had been a voice-mail message asking him to come fix something at her apartment.

"Why did you do that?"

It was time he came clean. "Because I forced her into this engagement. It wasn't real."

"Of course it was real."

"No, it wasn't, *Busha*. Trust me."

"Trust me when I tell you that I know real from not real."

"I had her sign a contract saying she'd pretend to be my fiancée. That's why I didn't tell anyone in my family about the engagement. I did it as a convenient way of…look, it doesn't matter why I did it." He shoved aside his burger. "The bottom line is that I've set things right now."

"By doing what?"

"By telling Serena that she doesn't have to pretend to be my fiancée any longer."

"She was not pretending."

"Of course she was—"

Wanda held up her hand. "Radoslaw, she was *not* pretending. And neither were you. You may have started out doing this foolish thing to get away from Heidi…"

"How did you know that?"

She patted his arm. "Your *Busha* knows everything. I could tell right away that something was up, that the engagement was not what it appeared to be. But I could also tell that there was magic between you and Serena. So I went along with your plan until you both came to your senses and recognized the truth."

"Which is?"

"That this is love. I know this is not what you had

hoped for, what you planned on. Not after Liza. But you must not run away from this."

"Marines don't run away from anything."

"Hah!" she scoffed. "They run from emotion faster than a prairie fire with a tailwind."

"Picked that up from Striker, did you?"

Wanda smiled but refused to be distracted. "Don't let this girl get away, Rad. You may finally have found someone who can be as radical as you are. You've met your match. Grab hold of her and don't let her go."

Rad didn't bother arguing with her, believing as he did that Serena didn't want anyone grabbing hold of her…least of all him.

Serena couldn't believe how the minutes dragged by as she waited for Rad. She had everything ready. She just needed him.

She worried that her outfit might be too much, or too little. A knock at the door threw that thought out of her mind. A check through the peephole confirmed that it was Rad. He'd changed from his uniform into jeans and a T-shirt. And he was wearing that sexy tool belt of his, the one that hung low on his lean hips.

Serena greeted him at the door wearing only a towel.

The sight of her made Rad long to take her in his arms, but he restrained himself. He was a Marine. He was Rad the Bad. Icy self-discipline ran in his veins. "You called to say something's broken. What is it?"

"My heart."

Her words stunned him for a moment. Then realization hit. The ice melted. "It's your father, isn't it? He said or did something…."

Serena shook her head. "My father and I have made peace."

"What?"

Serena quickly explained what had happened with her parents last night and this morning.

"Then why did you call me over here?"

The moment had come for Serena to tell Rad she loved him, but she momentarily got cold feet. She was also getting goose bumps standing there wearing nothing but a towel and a pair of silk panties. "Why did you leave me that message about breaking off our engagement and setting me free?"

"I thought that's what you wanted."

"Is it what you want? Did what my father told your friends embarrass you?"

"No."

"Then is it because of Liza?"

"What? What do know about Liza?"

"Not enough. Just that she hurt you. I'd like to learn more. Will you tell me?" She checked his expression carefully, looking for the telltale signs of his jaw hardening, or that grim chill of his eyes. Instead she saw…wariness?

But he said nothing.

Maybe he didn't have to. Maybe it was obvious to anyone not looking for a stupid silver lining that Liza was the woman he loved and that Serena wasn't. "That's okay. If you don't want to talk about it…"

"No. You deserve to know."

Great. She'd opened this Pandora's box. Now she was afraid of what she'd learn.

"Liza and I were in love."

Serena had tried to brace herself for the words, but even so hearing them still hurt. Enormously.

"She died of leukemia. We were high school sweethearts. We went to college together, then I reported for duty. I was deployed overseas. She didn't tell me about her illness until it was too late. I barely made it to her side before she passed away. I vowed that there was no way I was going through that kind of pain again."

"I can understand that."

"Can you? My plan was to avoid love like the plague. Then I met you. And you blew my plans clear out of the water."

"I did?"

"Oh, yeah." He reached out to trace a path from her shoulder to her collarbone.

"What my father said about my going to jail, it's true. I lied and took his car without permission and he had me locked up to teach me a lesson. I thought he'd done it to show me that he didn't love me, but it wasn't that simple. Anyway, I can see that it might embarrass you to have a reformed juvenile delinquent as a fiancée."

He tilted her face up to his. "Nothing could embarrass me about the woman I…"

Her heart stopped. "Yes? The woman you…?"

Rad stepped away from her, as if needing to put some space between them to maintain his calm. "I don't want to pressure you. After meeting your father, I can understand how important it is for you not to be coerced or bossed into doing something you don't want to do."

"Telling me how you feel about me is not being bossy," she quickly assured him. "Tell me." She moved closer and put her hand on his bare arm. "Please."

"I love you."

"I'm so glad!" Serena launched herself into his arms, which were opened wide to receive her. "Because I love you, too."

"In that case there's only thing to do…"

"Yes?"

"Serena Anderson, would you do me the great honor of becoming my wife? For real. Forever."

"Yes, yes, yes, yes, yes, ye—" Rad cut off her joyful acceptance with a kiss.

Six months later…

"Have I said how much I love weddings?" Serena murmured with a dreamy sigh.

Lucy rolled her eyes. "Only about a thousand times."

"I saw that." Serena shot her a chastising look. "You're not supposed to mock the bride on her wedding day."

"No? I thought that was my job as matron of honor."

"No, your job is to make sure I'm ready on time."

"I thought that was Kalinda's job."

Kalinda shook her head. "No way. She's my boss. I'm not going to be telling her what to do."

Serena turned away from the mirror where she'd been fastening the chandelier-style pearl earrings Rad had given her. Her hair was piled up on her head in an elaborate style that she was willing to bet Rad would take two seconds to undo once they were alone. "Okay, you two, tell me, how do I look?"

Because of the somewhat unconventional location of their wedding, Serena had chosen a simple but elegant duchess satin sheath as her wedding dress. The halter neckline accented the scoop neck that was trimmed with pearls. The short sweep train made maneuvering easier than a longer one would have.

"You look gorgeous," Lucy assured her.

"Do you think I'm crazy to be holding a wedding on the street outside my store?" Serena asked.

"I read in *Vogue* that street weddings are in this year," Lucy replied with a grin.

A knock on the door to her bedroom door prevented her from answering. "It's us. Wanda, Iris and Angela. Can we come in?"

"Sure."

Serena was deeply moved by how both Wanda and Angela had taken her mom under their collective wing. She was like a new woman, more confident and outgoing. Both her parents had gone in for counseling and things had improved dramatically over the past six months.

"Oh, my. You do look stunning." The comment came from Angela, her soon-to-be mother-in-law. Serena had felt at ease the moment she'd met her and Rad's father Stan.

Wanda came forward to clasp Serena's hands in hers. "My Rad is one lucky boy."

"We're the lucky ones, having you." Serena kissed her cheek.

Wanda blinked. "There now, you will be having me in tears soon. We came here to get things done, not to cry. Everyone knows their lines, right?"

Serena nodded.

"No, not you. Not for the wedding ceremony. I meant afterward, for the traditional Polish Sharing of the

Bread, Salt and Wine. The parents of the couple—that is you, Angela, and Stan and you, Iris, and Frank—greet the couple with rye bread that is lightly sprinkled with salt and a goblet of wine. You mustn't put on the salt until the ceremony begins. You remember your lines?"

Angela and Iris nodded and spoke in unison. "The bread represents our hope that our children will never experience hunger or need, the salt is meant to remind you that life may be difficult at times and you must learn to cope together with any struggles."

"Excellent. Then you give them the goblet of wine and Serena and Rad both take a drink and then you say…"

"We hope you will never thirst and that you'll have a life of good health and cheer," Angela and Iris said.

"Bravo. Very good." Wanda hugged them both. "I believe we are ready now."

"Aren't you forgetting something?" Angela said.

Wanda frowned. "What?"

"Something new, something old…" Iris prompted.

"Of course." The three older women turned to Serena. "You already have the something new." Wanda pointed to the earrings Rad had given her.

"But I hope you will accept this as something borrowed." She reached into her large purse to pull out a blue velvet box.

Serena opened it to find a delicate pearl necklace. "My husband Chuck gave that to me on my wedding day."

"It's lovely."

"And here's something blue," Angela said, handing Serena a lovely bracelet in hammered silver and lapis lazuli.

"And this is the something old," Serena's mother

said. "It's an amber ring that belonged to my great-grandmother."

"She was Polish, you know," Wanda added with a big smile.

Serena blinked away the tears. "Thank you. All of you. I don't know what to say."

"Say that you are ready to go downstairs and get hitched," Lucy said, pointing to the clock. "It's time to get this show on the road!"

"How the mighty have fallen," Striker noted with a shake of his head.

"Yeah, it's a pitiful sight, isn't it," Ben agreed.

"Affirmative," their youngest brother Tom said.

"You're the baby in the family, what do you know?" Rad retorted.

"I'm only a minute younger than Steve." Tom pointed to his twin brother.

"So you're both clueless," Rad said.

"We're both *single*," Tom said. "The last two remaining Kozlowski bachelors."

"Yeah, and we aim on staying that way," Steve added.

Both younger brothers had the same dark hair as their older siblings, but they weren't merely mirror copies of each other or of anyone else in the family. They were their own men.

"Rad claimed the same thing," Ben reminded them. "That he was never giving up his freedom."

"Yeah, well, I learned that freedom isn't worth much if there's no one to share it with."

"Aw, he's gone all sentimental on us," Steve mocked him.

"Your day will come," Rad warned him with a glare.

"So will yours," Striker said. "I decorated the limo like you did for me at my Texas wedding."

"Did you add one of your Texas-sayings bumper stickers too?"

"You'll just have to wait and see now, won't you?"

Rad was tempted to tell them that he and Serena weren't taking the limo to their ocean-side reception, that the groomsmen and bridesmaids were, but then decided he'd let them discover that piece of intel on their own.

"Are you ready?" Serena's dad asked her as he joined her at the foot of the stairs leading down from her apartment.

Serena nodded. Her father was giving her away and he looked distinguished in his dark suit.

"I..." He cleared his throat. "I…uh…I'm real proud of you, pumpkin."

Serena squeezed his hand and blinked the tears away. "Thank you, dad. I'm real proud of you, too."

And she was. He'd come a long way in the past six months. They both had.

"Okay, the music is starting," Lucy noted. "Go on, girls."

Serena's goddaughter Becky and Amy were both acting as flower girls. Both were dressed in cute white dresses as they carried a basket of red rose petals that they tossed onto the white carpet that had been laid over the asphalt.

Serena didn't appreciate how lovely the canopied area was until she got closer. The folding chairs, the same ones she'd borrowed from the church for her book signings, were covered with ivory slipcovers while trellises stood on either side, providing a natural wall of climbing blush roses in bloom.

The wedding flowers were done by Jane and Hosea, and they'd done an outstanding job—from the stunning bouquet they'd created for her out of red-and-white roses, to the displays adorning the dais where the minister waited for them.

Serena took a deep breath as she caught sight of Rad. He looked stunning in his dress blue uniform.

As she walked down the aisle on her father's arm, Serena noted friends in the audience—Heather and many other customers from the store, Ellie's friends and now hers, Latesha and Cyn, and even Clay and Heidi. But her main attention remained focused on Rad.

This was the man of her heart. She had no doubts about her decision to marry him. No doubts at all.

The wedding went by in a flash for her, yet she also enjoyed every moment of it—from the spring breeze that lightly ruffled her gown to the feel of Rad's hand on hers as he slid the wedding band onto her finger. And then there was the kiss—a culmination of all the love they felt for one another.

When the minister proclaimed them husband and wife the entire crowd applauded their approval. The Marines in the audience shouted *"ooohrah!"* as Serena and Rad made their way down the aisle.

Once they were outside, Rad hurried her away from the limo waiting and instead led her to the side of her...*their* building. "I've arranged for a more romantic mode of transportation," he told her with that slow smile of his, the one that lit his eyes.

"What is it? A Humvee or a tank?" she teased him.

"Oh ye of little faith. I thought I'd take a page out of one of those romance novels that sell so well in your store. Ta-dah!" He gestured to the horse-drawn carriage waiting for them before scooping her in his arms and depositing her inside.

"Are you impressed?" he asked as he joined her.

"Absolutely," she purred, running her hand over his broad chest before drawing his head down to hers. "Let me show you how impressed I really am."

"I think I'd like that, wife."

Their heated kiss was interrupted by the arrival of the crowd of well-wishers as the horse-drawn carriage began moving.

"My hero," Serena murmured with a grin. "My Marine."

"You've got that right."

And she had. Serena had gotten it right by marrying the man she loved with all her heart, the man who loved her back with honor, courage, and commitment. The Marine Corps way.

* * * * *

Watch for Steve's and Tom's stories coming soon from Cathie Linz and Silhouette Romance.

If you enjoyed what you just read,
then we've got an offer you can't resist!

Take 2 bestselling
love stories FREE!
Plus get a FREE surprise gift!

///////////////////////////

Clip this page and mail it to Silhouette Reader Service™

IN U.S.A.	**IN CANADA**
3010 Walden Ave.	P.O. Box 609
P.O. Box 1867	Fort Erie, Ontario
Buffalo, N.Y. 14240-1867	L2A 5X3

YES! Please send me 2 free Silhouette Romance® novels and my free surprise gift. After receiving them, if I don't wish to receive anymore, I can return the shipping statement marked cancel. If I don't cancel, I will receive 4 brand-new novels every month, before they're available in stores! In the U.S.A., bill me at the bargain price of $3.57 plus 25¢ shipping and handling per book and applicable sales tax, if any*. In Canada, bill me at the bargain price of $4.05 plus 25¢ shipping and handling per book and applicable taxes**. That's the complete price and a savings of at least 10% off the cover prices—what a great deal! I understand that accepting the 2 free books and gift places me under no obligation ever to buy any books. I can always return a shipment and cancel at any time. Even if I never buy another book from Silhouette, the 2 free books and gift are mine to keep forever.

210 SDN DZ7L
310 SDN DZ7M

Name	(PLEASE PRINT)
Address	Apt.#
City	State/Prov.	Zip/Postal Code

Not valid to current Silhouette Romance® subscribers.

Want to try two free books from another series?
Call 1-800-873-8635 or visit www.morefreebooks.com.

* Terms and prices subject to change without notice. Sales tax applicable in N.Y.
** Canadian residents will be charged applicable provincial taxes and GST.
All orders subject to approval. Offer limited to one per household.
® are registered trademarks owned and used by the trademark owner and or its licensee.

SROM04R   ©2004 Harlequin Enterprises Limited

Receive a FREE hardcover book from

H A R L E Q U I N   R O M A N C E®

in September!

**Harlequin Romance celebrates the launch of
the line's new cover design by offering you
this exclusive offer valid only in September,
only in Harlequin Romance.**

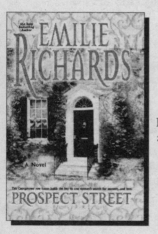

To receive your
FREE HARDCOVER BOOK
written by bestselling author
Emilie Richards, send us four
proofs of purchase from any
September 2004 Harlequin
Romance books. Further details
and proofs of purchase can be
found in all September 2004
Harlequin Romance books.

*Must be postmarked
no later than October 31.*

**Don't forget to be one of the first
to pick up a copy of the new-look
Harlequin Romance novels in September!**

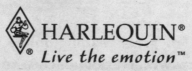

HARLEQUIN®

Live the emotion™

Visit us at www.eHarlequin.com

HRPOP0904

On sale now

girls' night in

21 of today's hottest
female authors
1 fabulous short-story collection
And all for a good cause.

Featuring *New York Times* bestselling authors
Jennifer Weiner (author of *Good in Bed*),
Sophie Kinsella (author of *Confessions of a Shopaholic*),
Meg Cabot (author of *The Princess Diaries*)

Net proceeds to benefit War Child, a network of organizations
dedicated to helping children affected by war.

Also featuring bestselling authors...

Carole Matthews, Sarah Mlynowski, Isabel Wolff, Lynda Curnyn,
Chris Manby, Alisa Valdes-Rodriguez, Jill A. Davis, Megan McCafferty,
Emily Barr, Jessica Adams, Lisa Jewell, Lauren Henderson,
Stella Duffy, Jenny Colgan, Anna Maxted, Adèle Lang,
Marian Keyes and Louise Bagshawe

www.RedDressInk.com   www.WarChildusa.org

Available wherever trade paperbacks are sold.

SILHOUETTE *Romance*

COMING NEXT MONTH

#1738 THEIR LITTLE COWGIRL—Myrna Mackenzie
In a Fairy Tale World...
How can plain-Jane Jackie Hammond be the biological mother of sexy rancher Stephen Collins's adorable daughter when she's never even met him? Ask the fertility clinic! But before Jackie gives up her newfound child, she might discover that her little girl—and the one man who makes Jackie feel beautiful—are worth fighting for.

#1739 GEORGIA GETS HER GROOM!—Carolyn Zane
The Brubaker Brides
Georgia Brubaker has her sights set on the perfect man. But when she comes face-to-face with her childhood nemesis, all her plans go out the window. The nerdy "Cootie Biggles" has developed into supersmooth, 007-clone Carter Biggles-Vanderhousen, who leaves Georgia shaken *and* stirred....

#1740 THE BILLIONAIRE'S WEDDING MASQUER-ADE—Melissa McClone
Billionaires don't make very good farmhands! But Elisabeth Wheeler is desperate for help, and Henry Davenport is strong, available...and handsome. Henry might not have any experience planting or ploughing, but he sure knows how to make Elisabeth's pulse race!

#1741 CINDERELLA'S LUCKY TICKET—
Melissa James
When Lucy Miles tries to claim the house Ben Capriati won in a sweepstakes drawing, he knows he should be furious. But he just can't fight his attraction to the sweet but sassy librarian. Can Ben convince Lucy to build a home with him forever?

SRCNM0904